Me vs. the Multiverse

Pleased to Meet Me
Enough About Me

ME VS. THE MULTIVERSE

ENOUGH ABOUT ME

S. G. WILSON

Illustrations by Aleksei Bitskoff

Random House New York

Text copyright © 2021 by S. G. Wilson
Jacket art and interior illustrations copyright © 2021 by Aleksei Bitskoff

All rights reserved. Published in the United States by
Random House Children's Books, a division of
Penguin Random House LLC, New York.

Random House and the colophon are registered trademarks of
Penguin Random House LLC.

Visit us on the Web! rhcbooks.com

Educators and librarians, for a variety of teaching tools, visit us at
RHTeachersLibrarians.com

Library of Congress Cataloging-in-Publication Data
Names: Wilson, S. G., author.
Title: Enough about me / S. G. Wilson; illustration by Aleksei Bitskoff.
Description: First edition. | New York: Random House Children's Books, [2021]
| Series: Me vs. the multiverse; [2]
Summary: "There's a rip in the multiverse that's causing chaos across dimensions, and it's up to Average Me, one of Meade Macon's multiple versions, to save the multiverse" —Provided by publisher.
Identifiers: LCCN 2020037420 | ISBN 978-1-9848-9579-0 (trade) |
ISBN 978-1-9848-9580-6 (lib. bdg.) | ISBN 978-1-9848-9581-3 (ebook)
Subjects: CYAC: Multiverse—Fiction. | Identity—Fiction. | Origami—Fiction. |
Science fiction.
Classification: LCC PZ7.1.W578 Pl 2020 | DDC [Fic]—dc23

Printed in the United States of America
10 9 8 7 6 5 4 3 2 1
First Edition

For E., W., and O.

Contents

1.	How Juvenile of Me	1
2.	Caving In	7
3.	The Impossible Fold	17
4.	Lunch Bunch	21
5.	Food with Felons	27
6.	Talk to Me	32
7.	Cave Math	41
8.	Trust in Me	45
9.	Dung Ball	53
10.	Me Con: The Return	58
11.	Take It from Me	65
12.	Vote for Me	71
13.	Absolute Zero	78
14.	TheME Park	85
15.	Ripped a New One	92
16.	Heap of Fun	96
17.	Fizzed Out	103
18.	Try to Trick Me	108
19.	Magic in Me	116
20.	Finals Fantasy	123

21.	Origamagic	128
22.	Macadamia Me	137
23.	Super-Size Me	142
24.	Change-a-Ball	149
25.	Playing Hooky	158
26.	The Chosen One	165
27.	Mr. Fartz	170
28.	Business as Usual	177
29.	Leave Me Be	186
30.	Mystery Me	192
31.	Mediocre Me	196
32.	Viral Sensation	201
33.	Flight of the *Titanic-Hindenburg*	210
34.	Please Release Me	219
35.	Make 'Em Laugh	226
36.	A Stitch in Time	234
37.	You and Me Both	241
38.	Get Me Outta Here	246
39.	Good Deed for the Day	253
	Acknowledgments	261

I

How Juvenile of Me

So this one time in juvenile hall, I went sleepwalking and peed on my cellmate Lil Battleship, the most dangerous kid in lockup.

Then my watch had to go and narc on me about it.

"This is not a good deed!" blared the robotic voice of the MeMinder X on my wrist, blasting the last dregs of sleep from my mind. Dad had built his latest version of the smart watch with a Good Deed Tracker, an app that read your pulse, temperature, and other vitals to sense a guilty conscience. He would have been thrilled to know his snitch-on-a-wrist could tattletale on me even in my sleep. But I saw no reason to celebrate: the stupid thing woke up Lil Battleship too.

"Meade?!" The groggy giant looked himself over, peering at the stains on his shirt. He touched the puddle of pee in his bed and sniffed his finger. Suddenly, he wasn't so tired. *"Meade?!"*

Eardrum and Slime, the two other juvenile delinquents who shared our room, started to stir.

"You peed on me?" Lil Battleship looked more hurt than angry, which made me feel even worse. Though he beat up other kids all the time, he'd never picked on me. We'd sort of become friends. Now all bets were off, especially as our audience woke up.

"He peed on you?!" shouted Eardrum. Most anything from his mouth came out as a shout.

"That's cold!" said Slime. "You can't take that lying down!"

If those two hadn't egged him on, Lil Battleship might have forgiven me. After all, I'd told him about my sleep-peeing problem, and he'd claimed to understand. I didn't go around telling just anyone what my bladder made me do at night, but Lil Battleship and I had bonded super fast over comics, cats, and the desperate need for a friend in a very unfriendly place. One time he'd confessed to me his love of weepy Hallmark Channel movies, so it had seemed only fair that I share a deep, dark embarrassing secret too. Since I couldn't exactly fess up that I'd traveled between dimensions in a hotel elevator, the next best thing was my stories of where I'd gone wee-wee at night. I just hadn't ever expected him to become part of another chapter in that saga.

Let's get one thing straight. I hadn't sleep-peed in years, not since the time I went in my tub of Legos as a kid. So why now? Why would I revert to my worst bad habit at the worst possible time in the worst possible place and on the worst possible person?

One word: stress. Being stuck at the County Youth Development Center three months into a long sentence will do that to you. It was a tough place filled with tough kids, and I didn't deserve to be there. I know that's what every prisoner says, but in my case, it was true—even if nobody in their right mind would've believed my excuse.

Two especially stupid and annoying versions of me from parallel Earths—Dare Me and Click Me—had posed as yours truly during a very public crime spree around my town. They'd littered the internet with videos of *me* doing graffiti, smashing windows, stealing stuff, and lots of other wholesome activities. Overnight I'd racked up a record more sizable than most of my fellow inmates combined, and the evidence was online for everybody to see.

I'd become the internet's favorite juvenile delinquent.

Though I'd never so much as shoplifted a piece of candy before, the judge threw the book at me. It hadn't helped that I'd run away from the cops when they'd tried to arrest me in front of my entire school. Sure, that resisting-arrest charge was on me, and, yeah, so was the breaking-and-entering citation for busting into both branches of the Janus Hotel. But

I'd had a good reason. Namely: saving the entire planet, plus scads of other alternate Earths throughout the multiverse.

But at this particular moment, I was just a bed-wetting moron who couldn't even manage to wet his own bed.

As Eardrum and Slime jeered in the background, Lil Battleship grabbed my shoulder. Not hard enough to hurt, but not light enough for me to shake free. Maybe at one time I could have broken his hold with the fizz, the mysterious energy that let me borrow the talents of other Mes. But the fizz had gone flat a long time ago, and I'd given up hope that it would ever come back.

Lil Battleship leaned in to whisper, "Look, I get it, you were sleep-peeing, like you told me about. But I can't let this stand. Gotta save face. So where you want it? I'll stop at one punch, but I gotta leave a bruise somewhere people can see. You want it in the eyes, the nose, or the jaw?"

"Decisions, decisions," I croaked. My words got drowned out by Eardrum and Slime chanting "Kill him!" over and over.

Then, just like that, they went silent. I glanced their way and saw what had shut them up.

A monster stood between them.

It was the general shape and size of a wild turkey, but with a few . . . extras. Instead of feathers, thick and floppy brown fur covered its body. Tusks—actual white and pointy tusks—poked out from either side of its bulbous beak. It was like some sort of mutated cross between a dodo and a woolly mammoth. A woolly dodo.

4

Eardrum and Slime both stood stock-still as the mop-bodied bird bobbed its head between them, pecking at their pockets like a pigeon hoping to score some crumbs. One of its tusks got hooked on Eardrum's waistband, and the woolly dodo tugged and tugged to get loose. With every yank, a soft whimper escaped from Eardrum's chattering teeth. By the time the bird had unhooked itself with a snap of underwear elastic, it was all too much for Eardrum: he fainted from sheer fright.

Slime started to scream, but a hand reached around from behind him and covered his mouth. Mud and fungus coated the hand and the rest of the figure it was attached to: a filthy boy who emerged from the shadows. Somehow, under all that sludge, I saw a familiar face.

It was me, if I'd had the bad luck to fall into the deep end of the muckiest, most bug-infested swamp. He wore nothing but a raggedy, stained loincloth and some twigs. A literal bird's nest clung to his tangle of hair.

I'd seen this mess of a Me before. He was Caveman Me, whose napping body Meticulous Me had tripped over when I dumped him off on a prehistoric Earth. If Caveman had somehow gotten here, that could only mean . . .

"Looking for me, mate?" said a voice beside me. My voice. With a British accent. I whipped my head around just in time to see another hand

squeezing Lil Battleship's shoulder. My friend's eyes rolled up into his head as he fell back into his pee-soaked bed like a tree falling to the squishy ground after a rainstorm.

In his place stood a Me I knew all too well.

My mortal enemy, my evil double, the worst Me in the multiverse. Meticulous Me.

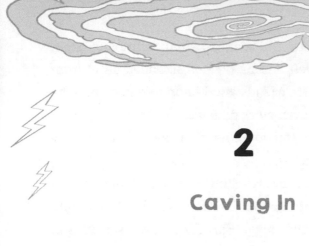

2

Caving In

Meticulous had picked up the paralyzing nerve pinch he'd used on Lil Battleship from Acupuncture Me. He'd learned countless skills from our other counterparts too. But there was one talent he'd come up with on his own and refined through years of practice: acting like a puffed-up jerk.

"Really, Average Me?" he said. "Sleep-peeing? Don't you think that's a little *naff* at our age?"

Meticulous was bad news all around. His early experiments with the origami drive had turned perfectly innocent Earth Zero into a multidimensional disaster zone. And rather than help all the people he'd displaced there, he'd started Me Con instead, a scam to steal technology from other Earths that left dozens of Mes stranded away from their homes. If my Me friends and I hadn't stopped him, he would have caused even more damage.

"Wha—What are you doing here?" I said, hating myself for sounding so nervous.

Meticulous walked over to Slime, who shook like a force-feedback game controller in Caveman's grip. The woolly dodo waddled up and down Eardrum's prone body and started pecking on the crud between his toes.

"Brilliant job, Cave! I'm very pleased!" Meticulous patted Caveman's head with one hand and placed the other on Slime's shoulder. He squeezed. Just like that, Slime slumped in Caveman's arms, dead asleep.

Wiping both hands on his knickers like he had cooties, Meticulous nodded toward Slime's bed. "Caveman, this is what we call a bed. Would you be so kind as to place this young reprobate on it?"

Caveman tossed Slime straight at his mattress so hard that the kid bounced right off and thudded to the floor. Pure delight spread across the filthy Me's face. He climbed onto the bed and jumped up and down, hooting with excitement. The woolly dodo ran over and joined him. The two bounced together in an explosion of squeaky bedsprings.

Meticulous shook his head like people do when a beloved pet does something silly. "Those two goofballs. Am I right?"

"Make them stop!" I hissed. "The guards will hear!"

8

"Quite." Meticulous shoved his fingers in his mouth and whistled.

Caveman stood at attention, drool spilling down his lips.

"Cave, put the body back in the bed for real," said Meticulous. "And do the other one too."

Caveman shook his head. Then, when Meticulous raised his eyebrows, he corrected himself and nodded instead. He hopped off the bed and shooed away the woolly dodo, who started munching the fuzz off Slime's blanket.

"What is that thing?" I asked as Meticulous made his way back over to Lil Battleship. "And what are you doing here?"

Meticulous crinkled his nose at the pee stains on my friend's clothes and sheets. "I'm going to need something to clean this up. What toiletries do you use on this Earth? Have the simpletons here developed deodorant lasers? Soap-bubble bots? Nano-scrubbers?"

"No, and don't act all superior about it," I said.

Meticulous adjusted the ruffles of his shirt. "You primitive Mes are so touchy about the dodgy state of your technology." He pulled from Lil Battleship's bathroom bag some toothpaste, a few chunks of deodorant stick, a handful of baby powder, and other ingredients, which he tossed into a bottle of mouthwash and shook up. Meanwhile, Caveman heaved Eardrum onto his bed, kicking at the dodo as it tried to nip at his bare ankles.

"Seriously, what is that bird?" I asked.

Meticulous poured his new concoction all over Lil Battleship's shirt. Somehow, it sucked up the stain and the smell in an instant. "Barbra, as improbable as she may seem, is the reason we're here."

The dodo snatched one of Eardrum's smelly socks at the foot of the bed and gulped it down. Her eyes bulged in surprise as the lump slid down her throat.

"What do you mean she's the reason you're here?" I said.

Meticulous dumped the rest of his miracle cleaner all around Lil Battleship. The pee and the smell evaporated in moments. "The Rip zapped her to Earth Three Hundred Seventy-Six. Remember that Earth, the prehistoric world where you stranded me?"

I still had nightmares about the Rip, a glowing green hole in the multiverse that Meticulous had accidentally opened over Earth Zero. It had filled the place with a mind-boggling mess of random people, creatures, vehicles, and even whole buildings from other Earths.

"But the Rip doesn't work that way!" I said. "It's only supposed to dump stuff on Earth Zero!"

"The Rip is spreading," said Meticulous. "It's spread to this Earth, obviously. How else do you think we arrived?"

"Quit lying," I said. "I would have noticed if the Rip had opened up here."

"It just happened. You were asleep. But you probably felt it on some level. Maybe that's what compelled you to relieve yourself on your bodyguard. What's his name? Tiny Warship? What kind of name is that?"

"Lil Battleship. It's his rapper name. Or it will be when he makes it big. And he's not my bodyguard. He's my friend."

"Stop fooling yourself. You only play nice to him for protection. I don't see what he gets out of the deal, but it better be good if he's willing to overlook how you took a tinkle on him. Now, about the Rip."

"Yeah, about that. How do I know you're not just making all this up?"

Meticulous waved a hand at Barbra, who pecked at Caveman's leg. No matter how much Caveman shoved the bird away with his grimy bare foot, she kept coming. "A woolly dodo isn't enough proof for you?"

"No," I said. "I don't trust anything you tell me."

He sighed and made his way to the door. "Then you'd better see for yourself."

The night sky looked like it had been poked by some humungous stick that left behind a nasty puncture wound. Streaks of purple swirled around a big hole in the air, with flashes of green light shooting out. Every few seconds it crackled inside louder than the world's biggest piece of Styrofoam breaking apart.

"This is not a good deed!" said the MeMinder, stating the obvious.

The dung beetles in my stomach rolled little balls of anxiety around and around. It had been scary enough sneaking past the guards to get here. But that was nothing compared to a giant hole in the multiverse opening up over my Earth. "The Rip is crackling," I said. "It didn't crackle before."

Meticulous gazed overhead with a peeved look on his face. "I hadn't expected another storm so bloody soon."

"Storm?! What storm?! Since when does the Rip do storms?!"

"When too much energy builds inside, the Rip shoots it out as cosmic lightning, for lack of a better term," said Meticulous. "If the bolts touch down on the ground, they'll either dump something from another Earth or take away whatever they hit and dump it somewhere else."

"How's that even possible?!"

Meticulous dusted imaginary fluff off his coat. "How to explain so a mind at your level can understand?" He clapped his hands together. "Oh, I know! Think of the Rip as a clogged loo. If you don't take a plunger to it, the transdimensional energy inside it overflows and spills all over the place. That's how Earth Zero wound up so barmy. I suspect that a stray bolt from the Rip is also what did in my second elevator."

My throat went dry. "You know about that?"

"Yes, yes. I saw the wreckage when we broke into the Janus earlier this evening."

The explosion. My mind went back to a nightmare I'd relived hundreds of times already. There I stood in the elevator bank of the Janus North, still choked up. I'd just said goodbye to Motor Me, Resist Me, and Hollywood Me, who'd left my Earth in Meticulous's new and improved dimension-hopping elevator, version 2.0.

12

The one that wasn't supposed to blow up.

I didn't even remember the blast, just the doors shutting and the gentle squeak of the car gliding away. Then I woke up in the hospital. My friends Twig and Nash had heard the bang from the front lobby and pulled me from the wreckage. They hadn't seen any sign of the other Mes, or even the elevator car. Just a big empty chute and lots of rubble. I'd worried nonstop about the trio ever since. I could only hope they'd reached another universe before everything went kablooey.

"My friends might be dead because of your stupid elevator and the stupid Rip you created!" I said.

Meticulous stroked his earlobes. "You're the one who damaged the control panel. It was part of the insulation protecting anyone inside from the erratic energies outside the elevator. So if anything, this was your fault."

"No way!" In truth, though, I worried he might be right. Had I sent my friends to their doom? How could I live with myself?

"Let's just move on," said Meticulous. "Aren't you curious how I got here without my elevator?"

"Not really. No." Sure I was curious, but I wasn't about to give him the satisfaction.

"I'll tell you anyway," he said. "I made sure that Caveman, Barbra, and myself got struck by the Rip. Isn't that brilliant?!"

Here's the thing about having an evil-genius double from an alternate universe. There's no avoiding the fact that under way different circumstances, you could have wound up like them. But that doesn't mean you have to buy into their evil-genius nonsense. "You let the Rip zap you on purpose?!" I said.

"Of course." Meticulous saw how confused I looked and sighed. "Obviously, that was the only way to power my portal paper."

"What's portal paper?"

Meticulous reached into his coat and pulled out a piece of yellow parchment as crinkly as a pirate treasure map. The paper sparkled as if it had been coated in glitter at a kindergarten crafts table. "It doesn't look like much, but it lets me get around."

"So you invented a new form of traveling the multiverse just to visit me?"

Meticulous tidied his hair. "Actually, I was aiming for *my* Earth. Still a few kinks in the system. And that's where you come in. Turns out it's right lucky we landed here, because you're the perfect Me for the job I have in mind."

"I'm not working for you!"

"Not even if the job is to get me home so I can finish the Stitch?"

"Is this the part where you want me to ask what the Stitch is?"

"It's a smashing technology I've developed that will fix the Rip once and for all."

The Rip thundered overhead. Caveman and Barbra huddled together in fright.

Meticulous scowled at the sky. "There shouldn't be a bloody storm right now," he muttered to himself.

"Let me get this straight," I said. "When we met, you couldn't have cared less about fixing the Rip. Now you're saying you were building a fix for it before you got stranded?"

"Quite. I've always wanted to fix the Rip. I just wasn't in a hurry. But now I *can't* ignore the danger. If it could snatch up this dodo creature from whatever monstrous Earth spawned it, there's no telling what other horrors the Rip is shuffling between other Earths."

"It could make all Earths like Earth Zero!" I said.

"Eventually. But I'll put a stop to that codswallop before it happens."

He walked over to Caveman and patted the shuddering Me on the shoulder. "There, there, we'll come out of this right proper."

"Oh, now I get it!" I said, watching the two of them. "Making friends with Caveman has given you a tiny ounce of human feeling."

Meticulous scrunched his nose like I smelled bad. Caveman aped the look.

"How can you say that about a fellow Me?" said Meticulous. "Aren't we all the same deep down? Isn't that what you're always on about?"

"I'm nothing like you!"

"Now listen. If you help Caveman and myself make it back to Earth One, I'll cut a deal with you. I'm willing to let bygones be bygones and overlook what you did to me."

"*You* overlook what I did?! What about what you did to *me*?!"

We might have gone on like this, but a bolt of cosmic lightning tore loose from the Rip and zapped us.

Trust me when I say that sort of thing tends to shut anybody up.

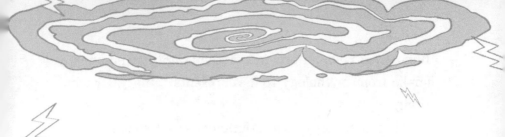

3

The Impossible Fold

Next time you nearly get struck by a bolt of cosmic energy shooting from a glowing hole in the sky, remember to close your eyes and cover your ears. I wish I had. I couldn't see or hear anything after the strike from the Rip hit the ground between Meticulous and me.

Hands grabbed my arms and helped me up. When my eyes and ears came back online, I saw Caveman at my side, propping me up with his smelly arm. Meticulous stood nearby, staring at something on the ground that hadn't been there before. An origami snake eating its own butt.

This was like no origami I'd ever made. Like no origami anyone on my Earth had ever made. They called it the

Impossible Fold, an origami of the famous tail-munching snake from mythology that represents infinity. Or something.

"The ouroboros," said Meticulous, awestruck. "I read about this in my origami research!"

To make a perfect loop like the ouroboros with a single sheet of paper, you couldn't just shove the tail into the mouth and call it a day. There wasn't supposed to be any break anywhere. That should have been impossible, like calculating pi to the final digit or finding a try-not-to-laugh internet video that actually makes you laugh. This origami wasn't supposed to exist, but here it was, fresh from some other Earth.

"It's impossible to fold, or even calculate," I said. "No origami artist has tackled it, not even cheaters like you who map out crease patterns on computers."

Meticulous scowled. "That's not cheating. It's preparation."

"Where's the art in that?" I said.

"Spoken like someone with rubbish math skills. Now open it! There may be a note inside."

Fingers trembling, I cracked open the perfect fold. Inside was a bad doodle of a unicorn, pretty much the way I might have drawn it. And below the picture, my crummy handwriting:

Make it here, pronto.

Ours sincerely,
Me

"Is this what I think it is?" I asked.

Meticulous peered at the unicorn from different angles. "It's obviously the origami key for the Earth this anonymous Me wants us to visit. Smells like a trap."

"Says the Me who trapped ninety-nine Mes at Me Con," I said.

Meticulous tugged on his lacy cuffs. "That was different. In any event, I'm not going to yet another Earth. I'm going to Earth One. And you're getting me there."

Ignoring him, I looked over the spot where the origami had landed, hoping for a clue about the mystery Me who'd sent it. There, in the dirt, I saw a charred candy bar wrapper and picked it up. BOWEL BLOCKER, it read.

"Motor Me!" I yelled, waving the paper at Meticulous. "Authentic Earth Eleven junk food! This belonged to Motor!"

Meticulous shrugged. "There could be lots of Bowel Blockers out there on any number of Earths. It's likely nothing but trash that got sucked into the storm and sent here."

"This has got to be more than coincidence. Motor's out there with the others, alive and safe. I just know it!"

Meticulous pointed to the sky. The Rip had shrunk behind the night clouds. "The storm is still on for noon. We need to focus on that."

19

How could I, or any version of myself, focus on the weather, with so many questions still in the air? Who was this mysterious new Me? Was it Motor? And if not him, then who?

I only knew one thing for sure: the multiverse was back in my life, whether I wanted it there or not.

4

Lunch Bunch

If the guards had had their way, they'd have forced all the kids at Youth Development to skip every meal, class, and recreation break until one of us fessed up to trashing the center. But state law required we be fed, educated, and exercised at specific times of the day, so there was no getting around breakfast.

That's why Meticulous and I were stuck in the canteen line together when we should have been searching for Caveman and Barbra. While Meticulous had been catching a few minutes of sleep in the common yard before sunrise, the prehistoric pair had snuck into the building and wrecked the place. It had been the quickest, most destructive vandalism rampage the center had ever seen. The canteen had survived countless hours of rough use by teen vandals, but Caveman and Barbra had reduced it to rubble in no time flat. They'd knocked over all the tables and chairs and scratched them up for good measure, leaving behind piles of trash and smearing the floors and walls with waffle batter, mac and cheese, and other food sludge from the kitchen.

The inmates were too busy gossiping about who'd done all this to notice Meticulous beside me. He'd traded in his fancy-boy clothes for a standard juvie uniform and slipped on a pair of glasses he'd found in a trash pile. It wasn't much of a disguise, so I made us take the last table in the back corner to avoid notice.

Meticulous picked up a chair and chuckled at the sight of teeth marks on its legs. "Oh, Caveman, you mischief-maker." He said it like a parent oblivious to just how much of a monster his kid is.

"How did you and Cave end up as friends?" I said. "I thought you hated all Mes."

Meticulous waved away the remark and sat down. "I don't hate Mes. I'm just annoyed with them for not living up to their full potential. To *my* potential."

I took a seat next to him. "I'm so glad to have your unique brand of positivity back in my life."

Meticulous chuckled. "Admit it, mate. You're chuffed to see me."

"Hardly."

"You mean to tell me you haven't been hoping beyond

hope that some Me, any Me, would come visit? Even a Me you hate? Just to know that a Me made it out okay?"

He had me there. I'd stayed up more than one late night worrying about my friends, not to mention the other Mes still stuck on Earth Zero. Since when was Meticulous so good at understanding how I felt? How any Me felt? Reading Mes was supposed to be *my* thing.

"That's right, you're not the only Me who knows what other Mes are thinking," he said, rubbing it in even more.

"Whatever." I looked around for the umpteenth time to make sure we weren't attracting any attention. "We need to focus on finding Caveman and Barbra."

"Agreed. We should be able to slip away after breakfast."

"Count me out! After this, it's visitation time, then classes. And mixed in there somewhere it'll be my turn to get interrogated about this mess. Really looking forward to that. 'Sorry, Officer, this is just another case of my stupid duplicates showing up and ruining my life yet again.'"

Officers O'Fartly and Pooplaski (real names O'Hartly and Poplaski) swore they'd interview each and every one of us about the vandalism until the guilty party emerged. They were already questioning Lil Battleship, who always got in trouble, even for stuff he didn't do. The poor kid never caught a break. Both parents gone, his brothers and sisters out of the picture, and his grandmother dead a month after he entered juvie. Given what he'd been through, I had no right to complain about my life.

Meticulous crunched a spoonful of dry cereal. He preferred his milk on the side, just like me. I hated reminders of how we could be alike. "I didn't come here to ruin your life," he said. "If I'd wanted revenge, I'd have gotten it by now. And don't worry, I'll protect you from your fellow inmates."

"Hey, I get by just fine here." I had Resist Me to thank for that. Among the videos Click and Dare had posted online was grainy footage of Resist beating up a bunch of Viral Mes during our rumble with them at the Janus. The video looked just enough like me to fool everybody into thinking I knew something about fighting, so nobody had messed with me. Not yet, at least.

Meticulous dug a fork inside his breakfast burrito, scooping out the insides and leaving the outer shell intact. This was one particular eating habit we didn't share. Maybe it was an Earth One thing. "Obviously, your internet reputation has shielded you so far, as well as your friendship with Petite Cruise Liner," he said. "But it's only a matter of time before someone tests you. And you don't have your precious fizz to rely on."

I tried not to look so surprised. "What makes you think I can't fizz anymore?" The truth was, I hadn't fizzed since the elevator blew up.

"Please. I'm a Me. I know these things."

I didn't see the point of lying. "Okay, let's just say the fizz *is* gone."

Meticulous smiled in triumph. I think he lived for these

petty little moments of victory. "I thought as much. You know what your problem is? You've lost what little self-confidence you once had. You feel wracked with guilt about what you did to me and the other Mes."

"You mean what *you* did to the other Mes!" I hissed.

Meticulous propped his feet on the table. "Plus, being cooped up here as a common criminal is getting to you."

"It's your fault I'm here in the first place!" I said. "And put your feet down! It's not allowed!"

His feet stayed put. "Is it my fault your legal defense was for tosh? Oh, right, you wouldn't know. You haven't earned a law degree like me. The truth is that on some level, you believe you're a bad person. You see yourself as more of a None of Me than an All of Me."

"None of Me? What are you talking about?"

He took another nibble of his breakfast burrito. "You haven't heard of None of Me? The Most Evil of Mes, as he's known?"

"I thought *you* were the most evil of Mes."

"Such a wit! None of Me was the bogeyman of Me Con awhile back, sort of the opposite of All of Me." He chuckled. "Remember how some of those prats mistook you for All of Me?"

They'd called me a lot of things at Me Con—including several assorted curse words—but being mistaken for the legendary All of Me was the most embarrassing of all.

Meticulous scooted his tray around the table with his foot. "Instead of a hero like All of Me, None of Me is thought to be a dastardly villain. Some Mes claim he's possessed by a demon. Others say he's a dark wizard."

"You mean there's an Earth with magic?! Cool!"

Meticulous slammed his foot on the table, shaking my tray. "The idea of magic is a daft fantasy! The multiverse and every Earth in it run on science!"

"You almost sound personally offended by the idea of magic."

"Enough yip-yap. Time is ticking. By my calculations, the next Rip storm hits in less than two hours. We've got to be ready."

"Not gonna happen. I have a big final today, and if I don't pass, I'll get held back in school. And I have my visitations coming up."

He sat up even straighter. "When you say *visitations*, you mean—"

"Twig. And Mom and Dad, of course."

"Oh." He tried to play it cool, but I'd seen that haunted look on his face before. His version of Mom had died, and he got touchy whenever she came up.

The silence between us might have lasted a lot longer if Lil Battleship hadn't come along to sit at our table.

Now I had to introduce my good friend, the most dangerous inmate in juvie, to my worst enemy, the most dangerous Me in the multiverse.

Things were about to get a lot more awkward.

5

Food with Felons

Lil Battleship was too worked up to register the fact that a barely disguised twin of me shared the table with us.

He launched right into his story. "So I'm leaving the interrogation room after getting the third degree from O'Fartly and Pooplaski, right? Then I see this messy-looking dude, all covered in flour and other stuff. Kind of looked like you, now that I think about it. Anyway, he's running down the hall, chasing this bird thing! Though it's like no bird I've ever seen!"

I shared a look with Meticulous.

"Uh, did you stop them?" I asked Lil Battleship.

"No way!" said Lil Battleship. "He was scary. The bird too. Anyway, they gotta be the vandals!"

"Where were they headed?" asked Meticulous, peering down the halls.

Lil Battleship seemed to notice my double for the first time. His eyes went from me to Meticulous and back again. If he was confused about what he saw, he kept it to himself. He held out a hand. "Hi, I'm Lil Battleship. You new here?"

Like most everybody when they first met Lil Battleship, Meticulous looked surprised to see such a tough giant acting so polite. "Quite. I just transferred in. So where did you see this dirty bloke and the bird?"

"They ducked into the supply closet with all the uniforms," said Lil Battleship. "Maybe the dude wanted some clothes. He sure needed them. Anyway, let's go explain everything to the guards. We can turn in the bird and the guy and clear my name. They totally want to pin all this on me. As usual."

"We can't turn in Cave!" said Meticulous. "Barbra maybe, but not Cave."

"Cave?" said Lil Battleship. "Barbra?"

"Short for *Caveman,*" I explained. "His, uh, nickname."

Lil Battleship screwed up his face in confusion. "You mean you know that weirdo?!"

"Uh, sort of?"

Meticulous eyed the closest hallway. "I'll go fetch those rascals. Think I could take out that guard with my tray if I threw it just right?"

Lil Battleship stood up. "You have to tell the staff the truth and get me off the hook!"

I hated how keeping the multiverse a secret meant disappointing everybody in my life.

"I'd like to help you," I said, the words hard as leather in my mouth. "But I've sort of got to help them more."

Lil Battleship gave me a look so cold that I would have preferred he'd just hit me instead. "You're no better than anybody else here. Selfish as the rest of them."

"It's not that!" I said. "See, Cave and the bird and this guy . . ." I pointed to Meticulous. "They don't really . . . belong here."

As I grasped for words, Eardrum and Slime walked up on either side of me.

"What's this?" asked Eardrum. His leaf blower of a voice blasted my eardrums. "You two getting your stories straight for O'Fartly and Pooplaski? Well, it won't work. Everybody knows you guys did it. I told them. And I let them know about the pee while I was at it."

Meticulous blew hurricanes of anger from his nostrils. "Will you turn down the volume of your voice? I'm trying to focus!"

Eardrum and Slime took in my counterpart. Surely they'd see the resemblance. My teeth chattered so much that they nearly guillotined my tongue.

"Who's this nerd?" said Eardrum.

"Yeah, nice glasses!" said Slime.

Meticulous stood, smoothed the wrinkles from his

uniform, and sauntered up to Eardrum. The cafeteria went quiet as every eye in the place turned to us. I slid down in my seat and covered my face with my hands. Meticulous had just increased our chances of getting busted by a thousand.

"You have a lot of words to take back," Meticulous told Eardrum. "The nerd comment for starters. Plus the accusation that my friends here vandalized this facility. As for the pee, let's renounce that statement too, shall we?"

Lil Battleship balled his fists. "Agreed. Take it back."

I didn't like where this was headed. Lil Battleship never actually started fights—he just had trouble backing down from them. One more strike on his record and he might get transferred to an even worse juvie than this one. There was only one way to break this up.

I threw all the food on my tray directly into Eardrum's face.

Egg, tortilla, hash browns, and Jell-O (because there always has to be Jell-O in any kind of institutional meal) splattered all over the loudmouth.

Shaking with rage, dripping with breakfast, Eardrum charged at me until someone pegged him with a stack of pancakes. I barely dodged a fake meat patty that sailed past my nose. Slime wasn't so lucky with the hunk of butter that splattered the back of his head. And before I knew it:

"Food fight!" somebody shouted.

A volley of yogurt tubes and orange juice cartons forced Eardrum and Slime to back off. A swarm of jelly tubs gave Lil Battleship and Meticulous cover to slip away.

I planned on sneaking out right behind them, but Mr. Lunt got to me first.

Yes, that Lunt.

My school sent my least favorite adult of all time to the County Youth Development Center once a week as part of some sort of feel-good outreach teaching program. I was convinced Lunt only did it to continue his life's work of antagonizing me.

"I saw the whole thing, Macon!" said Lunt, grabbing my arm. "I'm taking you to security. Hope you get out in time for my final exam. But don't get your hopes up!"

"That was not a good deed!" said the MeMinder.

"Now you tell me," I muttered.

6

Talk to Me

I might have been one of the few criminals in history who had to spend a good chunk of an interrogation cleaning up their interrogation chamber. Caveman and Barbra had rampaged through the conference room, and O'Fartly and Pooplaski expected me to deal with it. As I swept up garbage and refiled folders, my head was a microwavable popcorn bag of bursting questions. What sort of chaos were Caveman and Barbra getting up to now? What new fights would Meticulous pick next? What would Mom, Dad, and Twig think when I didn't show for the visitation? How would my grades survive missing the final?

I got so sick of worrying that finally sitting down to talk to O'Fartly and Pooplaski actually came as a relief.

"It all leads back to you," said O'Fartly, his broken chair squeaking when he leaned forward. "You're at the center of every stupid thing that's happened today. Lunt told us you started that food fight."

"And we have witnesses who say the rumble between your roommates this morning was your fault," said Pooplaski.

"And now we have evidence that you were behind all this vandalism too," said O'Fartly.

"Evidence?" I tried my best to sound innocent and surprised. I failed.

Pooplaski shoved aside a dented trash can to reveal rows of identical stick figures scrawled on the wall in marker. *MES*, read sloppy letters underneath.

"That's clearly short for *Meade*," she said.

"Anybody could have drawn that!" I cursed Caveman in my mind. "They're framing me!"

"Nice try," said O'Fartly. "The other guards say you're a good kid who just made a mistake. You know what we think?"

"Uh, you agree?"

He shoved a finger in my face. My nose filled with the smell of artificial breakfast pastry frosting. "We think you're a screwup who's just earned himself a longer sentence at a more restrictive facility."

Pooplaski nodded. "Sit right here while we write up our report to the supervisor."

They stormed out of the room, locking the door behind them.

Now it was official: in the span of a few short hours, Meticulous had ruined my life yet again. If I didn't get him and the others off this Earth, there was no telling how much more damage they'd do to me and the rest of my universe. I couldn't just sit there waiting for that to happen.

Searching for a way out, I tugged on a pull-up blind. It covered a one-way window looking out on the visitation room. All this time, the guards had been spying on us! Weren't there rules against that? I might have been outraged if I hadn't seen Twig sitting there waiting for me. Just the sight of her had a way of calming me down. Never mind that she was with Nash. The two of them sometimes visited me together, and I was okay with that.

Well, not really.

Twig and Nash were the only two people on this Earth who knew the truth about me, but things had grown awkward between us. And it wasn't just because I liked Twig as more than a friend, or that Nash used to bully me. People see you differently when you're behind bars, even when they know you don't really belong there. I was sure Twig and Nash already thought less of me, and they'd think even worse if I didn't show up to see them.

I'd started looking around again for an exit when Meticulous, of all people, walked into the visitation room.

34

He'd messed up his hair and was slouching in an exaggerated way. He was pretending to be me! Or at least, some amusement park caricature of me. He started joking around with Twig and Nash, making them laugh. They never laughed like that around me, not lately, at least. I saw a speaker on the wall and turned it on.

"We've been waiting so long, I think we only have a few minutes left, so we'd better say it now," said Nash, puffing out his chest. "We wanted to tell you about a new documentary project we're working on. The three of us are a team, though, so we need your sign-off on this."

Who did Nash think he was, talking like some sort of movie agent?

"It's different from the more newsy documentaries I've done before," said Twig, chewing on one of her curls. She ate her hair when she was embarrassed, flustered, anxious, or all of the above. "It's about middle school dances—you know, the teenage ritual of it all—"

"And we're going to homecoming together," Nash butted in.

The dung beetles trampled over my heart and nearly ripped it from my chest.

"It's only for the sake of the film," said Twig, chomping away at more of her hair. "Not a real date or anything. It's just to have the full experience of homecoming. But we know how it looks, which is why we wanted to tell you."

Nash gave Meticulous the winning smile he'd mastered

from years of, well, winning. "Exactly. We're all about com-munication. So, bro, what do you think?"

Meticulous examined his nails like they were more wor-thy of his attention than this talk. "Rubbish."

Twig spat out her hair in surprise.

"I knew he wouldn't be cool with us going to a dance together," Nash muttered.

Twig punched him in the arm, a move she used to re-serve just for me. Exactly how close had these two grown while I'd been out of their lives?

"I have no problem with you two going to some twee lit-tle dance," Meticulous said in a decent impersonation of my accent. "My problem is with Twig wasting her time on this sort of cack. I sincerely doubt the world needs a so-called documentary about a homecoming."

Twig raised her eyebrow to a 25 percent arch. I knew what that look meant: suspicion. His Earth One slang was giving him away.

"Her channel's lost subscribers lately," said Nash. "Something fun like homecoming is a way to build an audi-ence and get some eyeballs."

Twig scowled at Nash.

Meticulous chuckled. "The Twig I know doesn't give a farthing about eyeballs and all that tosh."

Twig's eyebrow arch went all the way to 100 percent. She was definitely onto Meticulous now. I had to put a stop to this before she outed him and blew his cover. But how?

The fizz. That was it. Meticulous had said my problem

with the fizz was a mental thing. What if I could get over it? I focused like I'd never focused before, going so deep into my head that the world around me disappeared. I'd always figured people who claimed to meditate were really just taking a fancy nap, but now I knew they were onto something. I could feel the fizz buried deep down in my gut, a barely flickering spark. So I reached out and touched it.

More fizz than I'd ever felt jolted through my body.

I passed out.

I woke up a few minutes later facedown on the tabletop with a thick wad of drool hanging off my mouth just like Caveman. The fizz had never made me pass out before. Then again, the Rip and its energy had never been so strong before either. It must have been too much for me to take, especially after such a long dry spell.

When I looked out the window, I saw that Twig and Nash were gone. Meticulous had moved on to my next scheduled visitation. The one with Mom and Dad.

They'd messaged me ahead of time that they had something "important to discuss" at this meeting, so I'd been expecting the worst: that they'd finally gone through with getting a divorce. They'd already separated a few months ago, and though they said it had nothing to do with me, I'm sure having a kid go full-on delinquent isn't exactly a cure for a troubled marriage.

Their T-shirt choices confirmed those fears: they wore different Doctor Whos. When my supernerd parents had a T-shirt battle about which Doctor Who was better (Dad liked the eleventh doctor, Mom the tenth), you knew there was a problem.

Meticulous held both their hands like some sort of grief counselor. "It's fine. I understand. I saw this coming. You two had a sixty percent chance of splitting up. Er, that is to say, lots of marriages end in divorce."

"Well, you're taking this a lot better than I feared," said Dad.

"Dad, would you pipe down for a moment?" said Meticulous, not taking his eyes off Mom. "I'm just glad you're both here and . . . alive."

I didn't have a say about anything in the outside world, and now Meticulous thought he could speak for me in lockup. That was the final straw.

Even a little trickle of the fizz went a long way, and the spark I grabbed passed into me like an IV of Red Bull. It raged through my limbs and flamed around my heart, which nearly Grinched right out of my chest.

I felt the talents of a hundred Mes inside me, but I didn't know how to use them. When I'd fizzed before, I'd operated on autopilot—Marathon Me's running or Bollywood Musical Me's dancing just sort of kicked in when I needed it. Now it was different. Because I'd activated the fizz on purpose, I figured I had to turn on the right skill too. I had the potential to do so many things—kick open the door like Ultimate Mixed Martial Arts Me, remove it from its hinges like DIY Me. Should I choose them, or some other Me ability altogether?

Stepping up to the door, I remembered the time I broke out of Lunt's supply closet by picking the lock. That had to have been an Escape Me trick. I hadn't ever talked to Escape, but I'd seen him breaking out of straitjackets at Me Con a few times. As I thought about him, the fizzing got stronger in my fingers. I reached for the door lock and had it open in moments. This was a first: I'd just fizzed a Me on purpose.

I didn't see any guards in the hall outside, but I didn't want to make any noise. I thought about Mime Me until the fizz went to my feet. Moving now in total silence, I tiptoed around the corner and squeezed behind a busted soda machine.

"This is not a good deed!" said the MeMinder.

I would have put the thing on mute if I knew how.

Before I could figure out what to do next, Officer Lenny walked into the room and called the Mom and Dad meeting to an end. I had to suffer through the sight of Meticulous giving Mom a long and teary hug and Dad a halfhearted pat on the back.

Lenny led my parents out, leaving Meticulous to find his way to class. As my double passed the soda machine, I popped out from behind it, hoping to surprise him. Meticulous didn't so much as flinch. "Hello, Average," he said. "Enjoy the show?"

"Why did you go in there acting like me?"

"I just figured you not showing for your visitation would raise a lot of unpleasant questions for Mum and Twig. And the others."

"You mean Dad and Nash?"

"Right, *them*. Anyway, too many questions might have complicated my escape plan."

I wanted to tell him off in so many different ways that the words wadded up in my mouth and nothing came out.

Meticulous slipped on his glasses. "You know, your mum is a lot like mine was. And the Twig of this Earth is very bright—I think she was onto my little ruse, but I can't be positive."

"You think?" I shifted to my British accent: " 'Oi! It's not bloody proper for you blokes to prance about together at the dance!' "

Meticulous rolled his eyes. "You and Stand-Up Comedy Me should perform together."

"Like your impersonation of me is so great. Would you just go round up Caveman and Barbra already? I'll meet you out there after my final and help however I can. But you've got to promise to go and never come back."

"Fine," said Meticulous.

But things weren't fine when we reached the door to class and looked through the glass pane. There at the blackboard, gnawing on a piece of chalk like a complete idiot, stood Caveman.

The most important final of my life was in the grubby hands of a brute who couldn't even talk.

7

Cave Math

Caveman chose to take the practical portion of my algebra final by filling the chalkboard with stick-figure hunters chasing down deer and buffalo. A furious Lunt grabbed for the chalk, but Caveman kept it out of his reach.

Everybody in class laughed and laughed except Eardrum and Slime. My roomies watched Caveman with sniper-scope eyes. I didn't see Lil Battleship in the mix. Where had he gone off to? Looking for me?

"What's Lunt, of all people, doing in there?" asked Meticulous.

"Never mind that," I said. "What's *Cave* doing in there?! That's my class!"

"Maybe one of these young scholars mistook him for you and invited him inside."

In the classroom, Cave bit down on a piece of chalk and blew a white dust cloud from his lips. Excited, he hopped up and down, spewing more chalk air. Lunt shouted at him, and Caveman blew an especially thick cloud up his nose, sending the teacher into a coughing fit.

"We have to get him out!" I said. "Now! If I don't pass this final, I'll have to repeat a grade once I get out!"

Meticulous beamed with pride. "This is math? Then you couldn't have picked a better Me to take this test for you."

"He's a caveman! You expect him to do algebra?!"

"Oh yes. Math is the universal language, after all. I taught him myself. Just watch."

Backing into the board to keep the chalk away from Lunt, Caveman finally seemed to notice the number problems written there. Excited, he started scratching out answers. Lunt looked just as shocked as I did to see him getting them all right.

Meticulous nodded his head in pride. "That's cracking!"

When he finished, Cave took a big lick of the chalk. The class laughed again as Lunt spluttered in wordless rage.

"Time to reel him in." Meticulous raised his fingers to his lips and whistled. Cave perked up at the sound and looked over at us. The filthy Me threw down the chalk, shoved Lunt out of the way, and rushed for the door. Eardrum and Slime jumped from their chairs to block his exit, but Caveman plowed ahead, knocking them to the floor.

"Like they weren't mad enough at me already," I muttered.

Cave slammed the door on a classroom full of shouting kids and one very angry teacher. Grinning from ear to dirty ear, he pulled Meticulous into a huge bear hug.

"There, there," said Meticulous, peeling Cave off him. "Glad to see you too, mate. But we've got to go."

The classroom door flew open and Eardrum, Slime, and Lunt burst into the hall. They started charging toward us but stopped short when they saw three variations of the same kid standing before them. As they wrapped their heads around that, we made a break for the common yard.

"Where's Barbra?" I asked Cave between gulps of air.

He grunted some gibberish at me.

"He thinks she's hiding close by," translated Meticulous.

We rounded the corner and reached the lounge, weaving around the busted TV, the shredded pool table, and the upside-down sofa to reach the exit door. The fizz in me had dialed way down, barely more than backwash in an empty soda can now. But I only needed a little in my fingers to work the lock and swing the door open.

"Took you long enough," muttered Meticulous as he rushed Caveman through the exit. "I could have picked that lock in half the time."

I hung back to look around for Barbra. Instead, I found O'Fartly and Pooplaski storming into the room with a pack of fellow guards behind them.

Pooplaski clicked a remote. The door behind me slammed

shut and locked tight. "Now, where were we before you cut our visit short?" she said.

"We were talking about the length of his sentence," said O'Fartly, closing in on me. "I think it's safe to say his time in juvie just got a lot longer."

An earsplitting honk filled the room. Barbra shot out from under the ruined pool table and went straight for O'Fartly's feet. He jumped out of her way, screaming. I couldn't blame him. Barbra looked even more bizarre than ever, junk food wrappers clinging to her fur, and an empty ice cream carton perched on her head like a helmet.

O'Fartly and Pooplaski tore down the hall in a panic with the rest of the guards. So much for their sworn duty to protect us delinquents from harm.

The latch clicked and the door banged open. Meticulous popped his head through the doorway. "See how brilliant I was with that lock? What did I tell you?"

Barbra loped through the exit, talons clicking on the floor. I didn't hesitate to follow right behind her.

8

Trust in Me

As soon as I set foot in the common yard, Caveman and Meticulous dragged a pipe organ in front of the door I'd just stepped through.

"Perfect!" I said, helping them steer the contraption into place. No guard would be getting through this anytime soon. Then a thought occurred to me, and I asked it out loud: "Where did we get a pipe organ?!"

"Special delivery from the Rip," said Meticulous, giving the organ a final shove. As soon as it slipped into place, Caveman and Barbra started slamming the keys, hooting with pleasure at the random notes they made.

In the sky above, the puncture wound that was the Rip

had gone untreated and gotten a nasty infection—bigger and darker than ever. A steady stream of lightning sparked inside it like some generator in a mad scientist's laboratory.

"The storm's brewing, all right," said Meticulous, shimmying out of his uniform. He wore his regular colonial clothes underneath. "Should be a real corker."

"So what am I supposed to be doing, again?" I asked.

Meticulous pulled out his portal paper. "This."

"And what do I do with that?" I asked.

Meticulous waved the parchment in front of my face. "Now, you wouldn't understand the science, but I made this from papyrus and treated it with minerals to attract the cosmic energy of the Rip. I need you to fold it into the right origami key for Earth One."

Coming from Meticulous, this really wasn't such a strange request. His elevator had been powered by the origami drive, which opened portals between dimensions when you folded the moldable energy inside it the right way. Not to brag, but I had a strange sixth sense about what those shapes should be. The right origami key for any given Earth would pop into my head, and my hands would do the rest.

"I don't get it," I said. "It's paper, not the green goop I'm used to working with."

"The portal paper is a vessel to collect and hold that *goop,* as you so delightfully call it," said Meticulous. "Think of it as a portable origami drive."

Lightning flashed above. Cave and Barbra ditched the

pipe organ and huddled together again. I almost felt like joining them.

"Why couldn't I have folded your portal paper inside?" I asked. "Why did we have to come out here?"

Meticulous searched the sky. "The Rip is drawn to the paper, especially once it's folded. It's like a lightning rod, attracting any stray bolt that shoots down. And we don't want any stray bolt."

"We don't?"

"Of course not! We need the storm's most powerful discharge."

"So I have to wait to do the fold until that special bolt is ready?"

"Exactly."

The Rip thundered overhead. It sounded plenty ready to me. "Wait a minute. You know how to do origami. Why do you need me?"

Meticulous smoothed his eyebrows. "I tried that. Watching the storm for the right moment while folding at the same time proved . . . distracting."

"So you wound up here by accident. Nice one!"

"Average, you may have many, many faults, faults too numerous to mention. But one thing that can be said about you, perhaps the only good thing: you're dead accurate when it comes to folding."

"Is there supposed to be a compliment in there somewhere?" I asked.

"It's not a compliment—it's a simple fact. It has nothing to do with talent and certainly not with intelligence. It's not unlike the way a feral kitten off the streets has the instinct to go in a litter box on the first try."

"I appreciate that comparison. Thanks."

"My point is that you're the only Me who can even come close to folding as precisely and efficiently as myself. So you'll do in a pinch while I complete the much harder task of analyzing the storm to find the right moment for us to make our move. Now, let me tell you the origami key for my Earth."

My mind fizzed, and an image appeared: "A growling riflebird."

Meticulous's lips tightened. "Lucky guess. Get ready to do the fold while I keep an eye out. Should be any moment."

As the sky rattled louder than ever, Lil Battleship, of all people, stepped from behind one of the basketball hoops. He pointed at Cave and Barbra, who still shivered in fright. "Aha!"

A bolt struck the ground ahead, raising a curtain of smoke between us and the exit door. Something large and angry roared on the other side. Claws as thick as swords ripped apart the smoke, and a huge brown monster burst through. It had the face of a sloth, the teeth of a saber-toothed cat, and the body of a grizzly bear on protein powder.

"Keep still and it won't notice," said Meticulous.

We watched, mesmerized, as the creature dug a small

crater in the ground with its claws and started licking up the bugs underneath.

"What is that?!" I asked.

"A giant ground sloth?" said Lil Battleship, forgetting to be scared. "Like from the Ice Age movies?"

"A saber-toothed sloth!" I said.

"Evolution must have taken some exciting twists and turns on whatever Earth this thing comes from," said Meticulous.

"Another Earth?!" said Lil Battleship. "So it's true! You two really are doubles! The multiverse really is a thing!"

I was almost too confused to return his fist bump.

Meticulous sighed. "Do you go around telling everybody, Average?"

"He didn't tell me anything." Lil Battleship grinned. "Not while he was awake, at least."

"I talk in my sleep?!" I said.

The Rip rumbled and Barbra squawked in fright. The sloth looked up from its bug buffet and noticed us for the first time. I don't know if it saw us as food or competition, but it charged forward just the same.

We sprinted for the big fence surrounding the center, Cave and Barbra leading the way.

The saber-toothed sloth gained on us with every thud of its paws.

"Why doesn't it move slower?" I said. "It's a sloth!"

Matching my pace, Meticulous shoved the portal paper into my hands. "Fold!"

My fingers ran over the glittery parchment, getting a feel for its flexibility. "Is the next bolt the big one?"

Meticulous looked skyward again. "It'll have to be!"

Cave reached the fence first and scrambled up it with Barbra under his arm. Juvenile delinquents tend to be good at climbing things they shouldn't, which was why this fence had bushels of barbed wire on top. Cave grabbed a clump like it was tinsel. He screamed as the sharp bits sank into his palm. He just hung there with Barbra after that, afraid to go back down.

Lil Battleship and Meticulous pulled ahead of me and made it halfway up the fence before stopping just under Cave's butt.

Meticulous called down to me when I pulled up to the bottom of the fence. "Why haven't you folded yet?!"

I was about to tell him off when a nearby voice cried, "Meade?!"

I'd been so focused on everybody above me that I hadn't noticed the people straight ahead. Mom and Dad stood with Twig and Nash on the other side of the fence, in visitor parking. My parents looked completely spooked at the sight of their son in triplicate.

Twig pointed at Meticulous. "I knew it!"

Nash nodded like he'd known the truth all along.

Mom and Dad looked from Cave to Meticulous to me. I thought for sure they'd realize the differences between us (Cave was still drooling, after all). I figured they could pick their true kid out of a hundred Mes, but they seemed clueless about which of us to turn to. They didn't know their own son anymore.

Just then, a bolt of energy tore from the Rip and shot to the Earth, striking Mom, Dad, Twig, and Nash all at once. The blast blew out my ears and scorched my eyes. But even after my senses cleared, I didn't see or hear any sign of them.

The Rip had stolen my parents and my friends away from me.

My brain was a spinning wheel on the screen of a broken computer. "Th-they're gone!" I spluttered.

"They just got sent somewhere else!" Meticulous yelled down to me. "They'll be okay! We'll find them! Just start folding, like we talked about!"

But I barely heard him over the roar of the sloth barreling toward me. In seconds I'd be a kabob in its fangs.

The fence rattled and shook as Lil Battleship jumped to the ground behind the sloth. He grabbed its tail and tugged hard, stopping the monster in its tracks. The sloth swung around and chomped those massive fangs at my roommate but only bit air as the monster lost its balance. Cave and Barbra had leapt off the fence and landed on the sloth's back.

The pair slid to the ground, falling beside Lil Battleship.

The sloth looked from one to the other, as if deciding who to eat first.

These three had risked their lives for me while I'd stood by the fence like a goob. I had to help them.

Meticulous must have had the same idea. We both charged straight at the sloth as the Rip roared overhead. As we ran, Meticulous pointed at the paper in my hand. "Fold us a way to Earth One!"

Sprinting toward a monster while wondering if your parents and friends have lived or died isn't the best situation in which to make origami. Instead of the growling riflebird Meticulous had wanted, my shaky hands produced some funky creature with three heads. Before I could go back and fix it, the Rip struck again, this time zapping Cave, Lil Battleship, Barbra, and the sloth into nothing.

I barely heard Meticulous scream over the roar of the next bolt, which struck the origami in my hands. Somehow, the paper sucked up all the voltage, so I didn't get fried. The thing with three heads that I'd folded turned green and glowy, just like the goop I'd handled in the origami drive. It hopped out of my hands and spun in the air, stretching flat like tossed pizza dough. In moments, it grew into a portal. On the other side, I could make out another common yard just like this one.

Meticulous rushed through the portal and pulled me along with him. "Did you make the right fold?" he asked.

As we stumbled into another Earth, all I could think to say was "Uh, close enough?"

9

Dung Ball

Getting zapped through an origami portal and teleported to a different dimension is hard enough without having poo thrown in your face. The moment I set foot on my first new Earth in months, *splat!* I was pummeled with a big hunk of soft and stinky dung.

"Score!" I heard a kid's voice shout. "You're out! Game over!"

I scraped away enough gunk to see that I was on a basketball court like the one we'd just left. In the same common yard, surrounded by the same fence, connected to the same juvie center. But that's where the similarities stopped. For one, the place was full of inmates on break. For another . . .

"They're plant people?" said Meticulous.

The kids on the court had ginormous flower blossoms for heads: roses, dandelions, daisies, and other plants. Their arms and legs were made out of stems and roots that had twisted together. It was like an entire botanical garden had clawed out of the soil to see what the surface world was all about.

As more poo slid off my face, I saw that thick and springy topsoil had replaced the blacktop, and giant Venus flytraps stood in for nets. But that was nothing compared to the referees. A pair of dung beetles as big as people clomped along the sidelines on their hind legs. They wore black-and-white-striped shirts with short sleeves that showed off their spiky insect arms. I could accept the idea of an Earth with bug people, but why did it have to be dung beetle people?

The larger beetle clicked its pincers in irritation. "What's that Me doing on the court?!" I knew that voice: Pooplaski.

"Hey, Me!" shouted the other beetle in the grating tones of O'Fartly. "Get off the court! You know the rules! Mes aren't allowed on this side of the grounds!"

Could these be alternate versions of my least favorite guards? Had I landed on an Earth where everybody I knew was a bug or a plant-human-hybrid person?

Then I saw the Rip in the sky. It had doubled in size. I'd only ever seen it this big in one place before.

"Earth Zero?!" Meticulous cried beside me. He'd avoided

getting hit by the dung. Lucky him. "This is rubbish! You brought me to Earth Zero?"

I shrugged, though that might have been my body shaking from nerves. "Is that where we are? I folded something with three heads by accident."

Meticulous pinched his nose, I guess because I stank. "You made a chimera?! By accident?!"

Oh right, a chimera: a mismatched monster for a mismatched world.

Meticulous pointed to a distant mountain with a giant face carved on it like Mount Rushmore. The sculpture wasn't finished, but there was no mistaking its subject: me. I'd been Rushmored. The Me up there looked infinitely more confident, charming, and focused than I'd ever felt. What had he done to get his face turned into a monument on a mountain?

"I remember my drone spotting that monstrosity the last time I was here," said Meticulous. "Something so daft would only pop up on Earth Zero."

"Who you calling daft?" bellowed a kid in ripped jeans with a sunflower head. Something about his voice sounded familiar, and not just the loudness. "And when did you jump in on the game? Dung ball is for dryads only!"

Dryads? Weren't those Greek mythology plant spirits or something? These kids looked anything but spiritual.

The dryads tightened their circle around us. Sunflower shoved me backward, and I bumped into the petals of a punk-rock tulip.

"Watch it!" Tulip whined in the unmistakable voice of Slime. This was a dryad counterpart to my hated roomie. That had to mean the loudmouth sunflower was Eardrum.

Slime grabbed my arms and held them behind my back with brittle hands that felt like the leaves of some under-watered houseplant.

"You can't go two minutes without getting us in trouble, can you?" said Meticulous, dodging the punch of a poison-ivy kid in a puffy jacket. Meticulous raised his voice to address the crowd. "Any of you blokes seen another chap who looks like us, just a little less tidy? He's traveling with an especially ugly bird?"

The dryads were too focused on beating us up to answer.

I tried to shake myself loose but worried about breaking their fragile plant arms. One wrong move and they might snap.

Meticulous didn't seem to share my concern as he yanked and pulled to get free of Poison Ivy and a tattooed hydrangea. "They survived, I know it!" he told me, ducking from Hydrangea's reach. "The Rip doesn't destroy things. It just moves them around. It either zapped our people to Earth Zero or sent them to another Earth entirely. I'm sure of it."

He almost sounded like he was trying to convince himself. But I had to believe him. The alternative was just too hard to face.

"The rules say Mes don't come on this side!" said Eardrum. "You Mes are supposed to follow the rules!"

"How do you know about Mes?" I asked.

"Duh!" Slime tilted his petals toward a nearby poster on the wall.

My own face stared back at me.

I remembered those clothes and the look of terror on my face. This picture must have been taken from a surveillance camera at Me Con while I was on the run. WANTED! read the title. IF SEEN, CONTACT AUTHORITIES!

Below my face floated a picture of Meticulous. No surprise there. What I hadn't expected was the Me at the bottom. A black hood covered most of his face in darkness, but you could still tell he was one of us.

"Funny, I didn't realize we were in league with None of Me," Meticulous said as four daisies in biker-gang duds overpowered him.

I looked around for help, but Pooplaski and O'Fartly just plopped themselves on their dung beetle butts to watch the show.

Apparently, the more things changed from Earth to Earth, the more they stayed the same.

10

Me Con: The Return

Meticulous tried to break free of the daisy dryads holding him, but all he got for the effort was a bunch of pollen up his nose. Face red, eyes fluttering, Meticulous went limp in their arms.

I got halfway through yelling out his name before Eardrum clocked me right in the face. The fizz poured into me until I was near to bursting. In a rage, I broke free of Slime and tossed him to the ground like some spindly weed. Eardrum took another swing at me, but I grabbed his arm before he connected. I tried to flip him over me.

Instead, I tore off his arm. It came free with a sickening rip. Green goo flew everywhere.

"This is not a good deed!" said the MeMinder. For once, I agreed with the stupid watch. What kind of monster was I?

Cursing up a storm, Eardrum picked up his arm and shoved it back on. Roots shot out from his shoulder and latched to his bicep, yanking it back into place. In moments, it looked good as new. Maybe a little too good. Eardrum punched his restored fist into his palm. "Hold him tighter than I did, boys. This won't take long."

Slime and some other dryads grabbed me again. This time, I didn't fight back. Just because Eardrum had fixed his arm, that didn't make me any better as a person. How could I live with myself after hurting someone like that?

Before Eardrum could take his swing, a lasso fell around his arms and cinched them in place. At the same moment, a volley of acupuncture needles whizzed through the air, hitting Slime and turning his shoulders into a living pincushion. The needles struck him in the same pressure points Meticulous used to paralyze people. In seconds, my attackers had been hogtied and frozen in place.

I followed the rope back to the hands that had thrown it. Cowboy Me stood a few feet away in his ten-gallon hat, holding the rope steady. Acupuncture Me, the familiar man-bun atop his head, paced the ground beside him with more needles ready to throw. The duo wore matching black suits and ties, sunglasses, and coiled wires drooping from their ears.

I didn't get why they'd ditched their usual clothes for this Secret Service agent look, but it seemed to help scare the dryads away. Not that they went far. The plant kids sank down into the ground below, going feet-first, deeper and deeper until only their giant flower heads poked out. The minute Cowboy loosened his lasso and Acupuncture plucked out his needles, Eardrum and Slime joined their friends in the dirt. The court had transformed into a quiet plot of oversize plants. Pooplaski and O'Fartly scurried away on their insect legs.

Without the dryads to hold him up, Meticulous keeled over, face-first. Cowboy and Acupuncture didn't lift a finger to help.

"Howdy, hombre," said Cowboy, no trace of a smile on his face. "What brings you back to these here parts?"

"And how did you break into this facility?" Acupuncture looked just as serious as Cowboy, like they were playing cops.

"Well, first of all, thanks," I told them, making my way over to Meticulous. "Second of all, we got zapped here by the Rip." I didn't trust Cowboy and hardly knew Acupuncture, so I figured the full truth could wait.

"What was Meticulous doing on your Earth?" asked Acupuncture.

"And how did that galoot get to your Earth in the first place?" said Cowboy.

I checked Meticulous's breathing. Seemed steady

enough. "It's all a blur," I said. "One minute Meticulous got zapped to my Earth, and then we got zapped here together. Other people got zapped too. Mom and Dad. And Twig and Nash. Plus others. Have you seen them? Did they end up here too?"

"We ask the questions round these parts, partner," said Cowboy.

Acupuncture started murmuring into his cuff mic.

"Seriously?" I asked Cowboy. "Why are you treating me like some criminal? And who's Acupuncture even talking to?"

"Don't mind these cats," said another Me who stepped around them. He wore a leather jacket with the collar up, blue jeans, and vintage 1950s sunglasses.

"Juvenile Hall Me!" I yelled, happy to see a friendly face. This Me had helped me out of a few jams. He'd even once held back Cowboy to let me escape Me Con. I could tell by the way Cowboy scowled at him that they hadn't exactly patched things up.

Juvenile Hall gave me a thumbs-up and a big smile. "Is Meticulous okay?"

I shrugged. "Don't worry about him. He's just Meticulous."

Grinning, Juvenile Hall tossed me a bandana from his

back pocket. "No offense, but you may wanna wipe up. Dung ball can be a stinky game."

"Thanks," I said, wiping my face. "What's with those plant people, anyway?"

"They're nothing but trouble, you dig?" said Juvenile Hall. "And believe me, I know all about trouble."

"And what's the story with the bug version of Pooplaski and O'Fartly?"

Juvenile Hall looked surprised. "You know them squares?"

"They're guards at the juvie on my Earth too, though they're in a slightly more human form. Ever so slightly."

Juvenile Hall laughed. "Sounds about right! Crazy, man! This place is juvie on my Earth too! So, does your juvie have a Lil Battleship?"

"Totally!" I said. "We were, uh, *are* good friends." I felt a stab of guilt thinking about the way Lil Battleship had saved me from the sloth before getting zapped. He had to be out there somewhere, and so did the rest of them.

Juvenile Hall must have sensed he'd hit a sore spot. "Listen, I heard what you said about your peeps back home, and I'm sorry, but they ain't made it here. Not that we've seen."

I held back a surge of tears. "I lost track of other people too. Motor and Resist and Hollywood. Plus the Virals."

"We ain't seen them neither," said Juvenile Hall. "But how did all this go down? When did you lose track of those cats?"

I gave him and the Secret Service Mes a rundown of the

elevator explosion and the weeks that followed, keeping vague about Meticulous. Revealing that the most-hated Me had invented a new way of making portals and a potential fix for the Rip might open a can of worms I didn't know how to close.

"I can dig your crazy story, daddy-o," said Juvenile Hall. "In some ways, us Mes have gone through something similar." He waved his thumb at the youth center behind him. "We're stuck here too, though it's not as much of a downer as you might think."

"You mean *all* the other Mes are here?!" I said. "Is everybody okay?"

"We'd better show this hombre," said Cowboy, taking my arm. He squeezed harder than he had to.

"Is that really necessary?" I asked Cowboy. I could have fizzed myself free, but after what had happened with Eardrum, the fight had gone out of me.

"Not cool, man," said Juvenile Hall as Acupuncture yanked Meticulous to his feet. My partner in crime could stand with help but still wasn't fully awake.

"We're all just thirteen-year-old cats!" Juvenile Hall continued. "Why you gotta be so square?!"

Acupuncture shook his head. "These two are wanted by the authorities and are considered dangerous." As he said this, Meticulous's head drooped and his tongue flopped out of his mouth.

"Yeah, real dangerous," said Juvenile Hall, snorting with disgust. He ran a comb through his hair.

"This is a mistake!" I said. "We didn't do anything! We only just got here!"

Meticulous lifted his head and opened his eyes to half-mast. "In a way, though, we never left! We're still prisoners!" He cackled like he'd had one too many liquid lollipops.

Acupuncture grabbed Meticulous by the chin and inspected his bleary eyes. "How have you moved between Earths? And why did you come to this facility?"

Meticulous giggled like this was all a joke. "Who's actually running things around here? I'll only answer to them, thank you very much."

Acupuncture straightened his tie. "You'll answer to me."

"Sir yes sir!" Meticulous gave him a sloppy salute. "Our orders are to put up with Agent Party Pooper until the real boss gets here. Sir yes sir!"

Juvenile Hall and I snickered. I even saw Cowboy's mouth curl with the hint of a smile. It was nice to remember that no matter what side we were on, most Mes found the same things funny.

"Come on, let's show you around," grumbled Acupuncture.

"Where are you taking us exactly?" I said as they led us to the door that, on my Earth mere moments ago, we'd blocked with a pipe organ.

Juvenile Hall gave me one of his slickest smiles. "Daddy-o, welcome to Me Con Two!"

11

Take It from Me

The moment we stepped into the recreation lounge and saw a bunch of Mes stuffing marshmallows into their mouths while running through every word from our fifth-grade spelling bee, I knew this was going to be a different sort of Me Con.

These Mes were laughing their way through the ME SPELLING BEE CHALLENGE, according to a sign hanging over their heads. The Mes across from them were having just as much fun failing at the Me Frozen Yogurt Challenge, which had them kicking jumbo cartons of vanilla fudge swirl with sprinkles (most every Me's favorite flavor) to keep them from splatting on the floor.

All around the room, Mes from the first Me Con hooted and laughed as they tried and mostly failed at other challenges based on our shared past. It was like the internet had personalized a batch of viral stunts just for us. Whirling Dervish Me nearly barfed up everything he'd eaten for the Fourth-Grade School Cafeteria Thanksgiving Lunch Challenge. Kabuki Theater Me and Pool Hustler Me had a whole audience of Mes in stitches with their moves for the Awkward Grooves Sixth-Grade Graduation Dance Challenge.

Watching it all from the lounge entrance, where Acupuncture still held me by my arm, I realized I'd never seen so many of my counterparts having so much fun. At the same time, I felt more apart from them than ever before. I'd promised to rescue these Mes and failed to deliver. Yet another of my screwups. How would they ever forgive me, or even accept me?

"Pretty slick, huh?" asked Juvenile Hall, standing beside me. "A lot more hip than that first Me Con. All we ever did was gab, gab, gab."

I shook off my self-pity and mustered a smile. "I'd call it an improvement for sure."

"An improvement?!" said Meticulous, still too weak to break free of Cowboy. "Where are the panel discussions? The dinner parties?"

"It was boring as watchin' cow patties dry in the sun!" said Cowboy. "Meticulous, your Me Con was more like a prison camp."

"Here at Me HQ, it's all about fun, you dig?" said Juvenile Hall. "We're free to do whatever we want."

"Within reason," said Acupuncture.

What struck me most about these Mes wasn't the good time they were all having, but the way they mingled. Mes had stuck to their cliques at the last Me Con, but here, those divisions didn't seem to matter. Money Mes laughed alongside Fit Mes. Play Mes goofed around with Alterna Mes. Nobody even seemed especially annoyed with the Silly Mes or the Chill Mes.

"Everybody's getting along so well too," I said.

"You can bet your saddle on that, hoss," said Cowboy. "We done buried the hatchet, by and large. Like the boss says, being divided don't do a lick of good. We're all Mes, after all."

"But you're stuck here," said Meticulous. "What if a Me tried to do a bunk?"

"What if a Me tried to escape?" I translated.

"No Me would get ten muskrats away from this place without the Earth Zero authorities picking him up," said Acupuncture.

"Muskrats?" Meticulous moaned. "Don't tell me you come from one of those Earths that measure things in units of animals! This is preposterous!" Meticulous tried to shake free again. He failed. "I demand to see this boss of yours!"

The other Mes in the lounge noticed Meticulous and me for the first time. They glared back at us with the same furious face, like we were watching them through compound bug eyes.

"So *this* is your idea of coming back to save us, Average?" cried Escape Me. "By bringing *Meticulous* with you?"

Meticulous waved his free hand to the crowd with the swagger of a grand marshal at a parade. That only made the Mes angrier. They shouted out the worst alternate-Earth insults I'd ever heard: "Leprechaun breath!" "Vase face!" "Bologna snatcher!"

I could have told them I'd been stuck on Earth Ninety-Nine and had no way of coming back, but they wouldn't have believed me. I deserved their hate anyway.

But did I deserve the beating they had to be planning for us? These same Mes had been quick to fight before, and as they started crowding around us, I fully expected things to come to blows again. The fizz came rushing in, and as I plotted my attack, I forgot all about what I'd done to Eardrum the dryad. I could fizz the fighting skills of Resist Me, or the strength of Mobster Me, or the insult comedy of Troll Me.

Pumped up on transdimensional adrenaline, I yanked myself free of Acupuncture and turned to Meticulous, who busted loose from Cowboy.

"Whatever these Mes have to dish out, I'm ready for it!" I said.

"Quite!" said Meticulous, sliding up his sleeves.

"This is not a good deed!" said the MeMinder X.

"Shove it!" Meticulous and I said at the same time.

Then some sort of goo splatted the back of my head. It dribbled down my neck and oozed across my shoulders. Meticulous got hit by the same gunk. We'd been covered in glowing purple slime.

All the Mes started laughing. Even Military School Me and Eagle Scout Me joined in, and they barely had a sense of humor. I turned around to see that Ultimate Mixed Martial Arts Me and Restless Leg Me had snuck up from behind to douse us with buckets labeled GODZILLA SNOT BUCKET CHALLENGE.

As the fizz died down in me, I felt like an idiot. I'd expected the worst of the Mes, and all they'd had in mind was a prank. A pretty good prank, though Meticulous didn't see it that way.

Scraping the goo off his coat, he looked madder than ever. "This will never come out!"

"Don't get bent out of shape," said Pool Hustler Me. "We've been using this stuff as a cleaner."

"It might even clear up the smell of whatever Average fell into," said Aqua Aerobics Me.

Everybody laughed. Even I had to admit that was a good one. Meticulous still wasn't amused. He might have taken a swipe at Ultimate Mixed Martial Arts Me if a new Me hadn't stepped into the room.

He had to be the boss we'd heard about. It wasn't just the suit and expensive haircut that made him look like a leader. It was the way he carried himself: commanding and confident yet warm and approachable, the way a president can go straight from ordering a bombing strike on another country to overseeing the White House Easter Egg Roll.

At the sight of him, every Me in the place burst into applause. They even started chanting, "Prez! Prez!"

So he *was* some sort of president. Or at least, a very presidential sort of Me.

Meticulous looked annoyed to be upstaged by this new arrival. "Oh, great, it's *him*," he said.

"You know him?" I whispered.

"I know of him," said Meticulous. "We've never talked. It might be a touch awkward, seeing as how I more or less ruined his Earth."

"You mean . . ." I trailed off, piecing together the truth.

"Isn't it obvious?" said Meticulous. "He's the Me whose face is carved on the side of the mountain. He's the native Me of Earth Zero. He's the elected leader of this barmy place. He's President Me."

12

Vote for Me

Like some charming male model in a clothing ad, President Me slid back the sleeve of his jacket to reveal a sleek MeMinder that made the MeMinder X look like a sundial in comparison. Prez tapped the face of the watch, and a cone of blinding green light shot out, beaming a sheet of holographic paper in front of him. He snatched it from the air and folded it with the quickest origami hands I'd ever seen. In moments, he shaped the glowing paper into a microphone. After a few seconds, the glow went away and he held a solid mic in his hand.

"A portable three-D origami printer," whispered Meticulous. "How lush."

"Where'd he get a MeMinder that does *that*?!" I whispered back. "Mine just nags me when I eat too many potato chips."

Prez made the universal sign for *quiet down* to the crowd of adoring Mes. "Come on, guys," he said into the mic, which boosted his voice from some internal speaker. "That's hardly necessary. You Mes are the real stars! I mean, look at how well you're mastering your Me challenges!"

Everybody laughed.

"Rubbish," muttered Meticulous.

"You almost sound jealous, daddy-o," said Juvenile Hall. "Is that why you never invited Prez to Me Con? Because he's a more accomplished cat than you?"

Meticulous just glowered at him.

"Now," Prez continued, "as for these Mes you've covered in Godzilla snot . . ."

The crowd booed, and Prez gave them a disapproving look. "I hear what you're saying, but let's have none of that, please. Remember what I always say?"

Everyone murmured the words together: "Always respect Me."

I felt chills seeing Prez hold the audience in the palm of his hand like this. I'd never imagined a Me could be so amazing. After spending the past few months as the internet's number one delinquent, I'd been more likely to believe in a None of Me than a President Me. But here he was.

"Very good," Prez continued. "I don't believe you were respecting these two by surprising them like that. But I also think they can respect you in turn by letting it slide. Right, you two? Can you let it slide?"

A little dazed from all those identical sets of eyes on me, I nodded. Meticulous started to say something I knew would be snarky, so I elbowed him in the ribs. He took the hint and piped down.

"Excellent," said Prez. "Cowboy, Acupuncture, would you both be so kind as to step away from our new friends, please? No need to intimidate them like that."

Acupuncture looked like he'd just had his healing crystals taken away. "But they're wanted criminals! And they have a lot of bad karma!"

Prez raised his voice for the whole crowd to hear. "You know what we Mes say in situations like this. Remember, everybody?"

Everyone chanted as one: "Trust in Me."

Meticulous narrowed his eyes. "Never fancied you for a cult leader."

Prez laughed. "Hardly. I didn't even want to be called President Me. It just became a thing. So, you must be the famous—"

"Meticulous Me," said Cowboy. "He's the yellow-bellied burro who made the Rip in the first place!"

Meticulous raised his hands to the audience like he'd just been introduced to an adoring crowd at a concert. "Why, yes, I am, as a matter of fact, known as Meticulous." Somebody, probably a Silly Me, beamed him in the face with a spitwad.

Prez turned to me. "And you're the legendary All of Me."

My face went hot. Some of the Mes here had thought of me as the mythical hero. Look where that kind of thinking had gotten them. "I just prefer to go by Average Me."

Meticulous snorted. "Mr. Humility. Now then, we have questions."

"And I'll answer all of them," said Prez. "But first, a few pressing matters."

"Such as our status as wanted criminals?" said Meticulous.

"It's a *huge* misunderstanding!" I cried, sounding more whiny than I meant to. "We can explain! For starters, the elevator blew up and we couldn't even get here until now. And then the Rip—"

"Don't debase yourself like that!" said Meticulous. "Prez isn't looking for an explanation. He needs us captured to show everybody he's an effective leader. This is just politics, plain and simple. Isn't that right, *Mr. Commander in Chief*?"

Only Meticulous could make the most important title in the country sound like a dis. Every Me in the place turned to Prez with the same look of anticipation, wondering how he'd react.

Prez simply smiled back at us. "I'm not arresting you at all. I don't mean to hand you over to the government."

"But you *are* the government!" said Meticulous.

Acupuncture whipped out one of his

74

needles and shoved it just under Meticulous's nose. "He was, until your Rip cost him the job!"

Prez shooed Acupuncture away. "Now, now, stand down, please. That's water under the fridge."

"You mean water under the bridge?" I blurted.

"Different Earth, different idioms," muttered Meticulous. "Try and bloody well keep up, would you?"

Prez chuckled. "You two are hilarious. Anyway, it's true: I'm not president here anymore."

"But he was the last cat to hold the position," said Juvenile Hall. "Before the council took over."

"So let me guess," said Meticulous. "After Average and I left and Me Con ended, the Mes got blamed for the Rip. Public opinion turned against you, Prez, and you had to leave office in disgrace. Rather than elect a new president, Earth Zero dissolved your entire system of government, replacing it with a ruling council that better represents the new populations who've been dumped here by the Rip."

To any other Me, recounting their greatest failure might have been painful. But Prez beamed at Meticulous like he deserved a medal. "Impressive guesswork! You're right on the bunny!"

Right on the money, I wanted to say. Instead, I asked, "Weren't you a little young to be president? On my Earth, people have to wait until they're really old to be president, like in their thirties."

"What can I say?" said Prez. "Age just isn't a barrier to doing stuff on my Earth. I became president at age twelve."

75

"And did a really rockin' and groovin' job too!" said Juvenile Hall Me.

The crowd whooped and hollered.

Prez just shrugged. "I tried my best. Like any Me would."

"But I cost you your job," said Meticulous, sounding almost desperate for a fight. "Arresting me is a revenge thing, right? You want payback."

"I can't blame you for an accident," said Prez. "In any event, there's another saying we Mes have been practicing. What is it, everybody?"

"Forgive Me!" the Mes chanted together. This time, though, they sounded a lot less enthusiastic.

"That's right!" said Prez. "It's all good, Meticulous. No worries. And that reminds me, I'd better check in with the council. They'll want to hear the latest."

Prez tapped his MeMinder again, and light beamed from its face.

"You've fit a portable holo-projector in there too?" said Meticulous, trying not to sound impressed. "I don't remember tech being so advanced last time I came here."

"It's something I've developed on my own," said Prez. "Since I left office, I've had more free time for research. I'm sure you know how it is, as a scientist yourself."

Meticulous kept his face neutral, but I could see the scowl lurking just under the surface.

The light from the MeMinder formed into the hologram of four people sitting at a table and staring back at us. Actually, *people* may not be the best word to describe the hairy

brown Bigfoot, the elderly lizard woman, and the blob creature whose body seemed to be made entirely out of Bubble
Wrap. The other member of the group was a human, but
just barely: he was an alternate version of Lunt, dressed in
the ugliest holiday sweater in the multiverse. Why would
they let any Lunt on a ruling council, especially a Lunt
dressed like that?

Another human scurried into the frame to take a seat at
the table. In the span of a single beat, my heart did a circus
tightrope routine inside my chest as I recognized her.

Twig had made it to Earth Zero after all!

13

Absolute Zero

The hologram of Twig looked smart and confident as she took a seat with the ruling council of Earth Zero. Why was she sitting with them, and where had she picked up that business suit?

"Sorry I'm late," she said. "A lake made entirely of pancake syrup just got zapped into the middle of New Chicago and flooded downtown. I had to approve the cleanup funds and lost track of mime."

Lost track of time. Was the mangling of clichés contagious here?

"This is the Twig of my Earth, everybody," Prez announced to the Mes. "The only native Earth Zeroan on the council. And she's doing terrific work!"

I should have realized that if Earth Zero had the space for a spare Lunt in an ugly holiday sweater, there'd be room for a different version of Twig too.

Embarrassed, she gave us all an uncomfortable little wave. "Thanks for the vote of confidence, Mr. President."

"He's not president anymore," muttered Lunt.

Twig rolled her eyes. "It's just a sign of respect. Don't read anything into it, Council Member Lunt."

"I have a question for the honorable Lunt," said Meticulous.

Lunt grinned. "Yes?"

"Good sir, could you explain what inspired you to wear that preposterous sweater?"

I couldn't help but laugh, and neither could most of the Mes in the crowd. Mes loved a good joke at Lunt's expense. Even Prez had to hide his grin.

Lunt's face turned as red as the squiggly patterns on his sweater. "How many times do I have to explain?! This is considered year-round formal wear on my Earth of origin! Which Me are you, anyway? Rude Me?"

Lunt waited for laughs that never came. Then he peered closer at Meticulous. "It's you, isn't it!? I've seen you on the posters! You're the Me who made the Rip!"

The other council members sat up straighter in their seats.

Lunt pointed a holographic finger at me. "And you're the other one, the accomplice!"

"I'm no accomplice of Meticulous!" I said. "I don't even like him!"

Meticulous nodded. "Feeling's mutual."

Lunt tapped on a screen in front of him. "I'll arrange a prison transfer immediately!"

"And I'll make arrangements for a fair trial too," said Twig. "Remember, everyone, they're innocent until proven guilty."

I didn't deserve a friend like Twig, no matter what version of her the multiverse sent my way.

"Sure, sure, a fair trial," said Lunt. "But they'll await that trial in the new maximum-security prison that just arrived from Earth Twelve, Build-A-Bear Workshop Alcatraz."

"Not so fast," said Prez. "If you'll refresh yourselves on the laws that were drawn up concerning the detention of Mes, you'll see in clause E, subsection 12.A76, that I reserve the right to detain any Me as I see fit. I'm invoking this special exemption now."

"Special exemption?!" said another person who stepped into the holographic room. It was Nash, dressed in a military uniform splattered with medals. "You'll turn him over to us now! Beggars can't be bruisers!"

"Sorry, General Nash," said Prez, not sounding sorry at all. "But I'm afraid my special exemption is the new law of the land."

"Negative!" Nash shouted. "Turn them over now!"

Mes all around us wilted from the roar of Nash's voice. None of us could shake our deep, dark fear of Nash, not even Meticulous. His left eye started twitching.

Prez, on the other hand, had no problem giving it right back to the bully. "You really need to get over yourself, General. It's not like they're going anywhere."

"You need them for information, don't you?" said Nash. "For the experiments you've been doing!"

"Experiments?" said Prez. "I don't know what you're talking about."

"Don't give me that!" barked Nash. "The havoc caused by the Rip is getting worse than ever! Just look at the latest rearrangements to Earth Zero's geography!"

Nash pressed a button on the table before him, and a screen popped up, showing a satellite map of the world. The land looked like an atlas that had been ripped up and glued back together the wrong way. A jungle butted up against an iceberg. A swamp oozed in the middle of a desert.

"These changes occurred in just the last week!" said Nash.

"And the syrup lake in Chicago that Twig mentioned is just one of many troubling reports I've received," said Lunt. "Yesterday, the Rip covered the entirety of Amsterdam in discarded friendship bracelets!"

"The Rip's getting worse!" said Nash. "And we're certain you Mes and your experiments have everything to do with it! The writing's on the stall!"

"Well, we need to ask you questions about it, at least," said Twig. "No one's accusing anybody of criminal wrong-doing. We're just trying to get to the bottom of it all."

"You're going to turn over those rogue Mes *and* you're going to report about these unauthorized experiments you've been doing!" said Nash. "You have six hours to comply. Then I send over a fleet to take away everything you've been hiding!"

Nash had more to say, but Prez tapped the MeMinder and the hologram disappeared. All the Mes cheered, and I joined in. Meticulous looked at me like I'd betrayed him.

"Thanks for not turning us over," I said to Prez.

He waved away my words. "It was nothing. We Mes have to stick together, right?"

"But won't it get you in trouble?" said Meticulous, clearly not in the mood for thank-yous. "That gung ho version of Nash threatened to send in his troops."

"Those squares will forget all about their trouble with us Mes when they see what we got cooking up," said Juvenile Hall.

"You mean the experiments that Nash mentioned?" I asked.

Prez gave us a smile so winning,

I could see how he'd charmed Earth Zero into letting him run the place. He turned to the crowd. "My fellow Mes, with the help of Meticulous and Average, we're now officially entering an exciting new phase! These two hold the key to traveling the multiverse. They're going to share it with us. And then you're all going home!"

Everyone cheered louder than ever. It might have gone on for a while if Prez's MeMinder hadn't turned on again. Another hologram shot out of the watch: the hooded face of None of Me. The crowd gasped. I couldn't blame them. I got a chill just looking at this mysterious Me, but I couldn't pull my eyes away either. Like Prez, he sucked up the attention in the room.

"Stop your experiments with the Rip or you'll pay the price," said None of Me.

And that was it. The hologram disappeared, leaving behind a room of very freaked-out Mes.

Prez raised his hands to quiet everyone down. "So now we know the infamous None of Me is real. But you know what? Why should we be afraid of him? Are we gonna let ourselves get pushed around like that?"

Nearly a hundred cries of "No!" rang out from the crowd.

"Is he pushing us around, though?" Meticulous asked me over the roar of Mes. "I heard it as more of a general warning. *Leave the Rip alone or it goes kablooey.*"

What did it say about me that I was thinking along the same lines as Meticulous? And that I was willing to give

None of Me the benefit of the doubt? If I was sympathizing with the bad Mes, did that make me bad too?

"We won't be bullied!" shouted Prez to more cheers. "No council, no Nash, and not even None of Me will stop *this Me* from getting all of you home!"

14

TheME Park

Call me anxious, but I could never step on a skateboard or hop on a BMX without imagining, at least for a second, all the ways I could die. That's why it didn't do me any good to see the Mes outside the front entrance of Me HQ throwing themselves into some of the most dangerous leisure activities the multiverse had to offer. They raced through the loops and tunnels of a hover go-cart track, jet-packed over a volcano, suction-cup-climbed an office tower, and on and on, in an endless display of reckless fun. Part of me was horrified. The other part wanted to join in.

Prez, Juvenile Hall, and the Secret Service Mes had led us out here to show off how they'd turned a drab parking lot into a theme park of rides from other Earths. They'd also wanted us to visit the showers at the base of a three-story water slide to wash off the dung and Godzilla snot.

"Like it?" said Prez. He had to yell over the screams of the Mes speeding face-first down the slide. "This equipment is the best outdoor entertainment the Rip has to offer. The best the *multiverse* has to offer. And a little entertainment keeps up morale, I've found."

"Which is important when you're locking up Mes," said Meticulous from behind his shower curtain.

"It's not like you have room to talk, Meticulous," I said, washing the last of the dung from my face. "You locked us up at the first Me Con."

Meticulous ignored my comment. "So you keep them distracted with all these bits and bobs to take their mind off their prison sentence?"

Acupuncture threw a towel at Meticulous harder than he needed to.

"It's a shame, really," said Prez. "The council sees Mes as dangerous criminals who need to be locked up. So we've had to play along and stay here under shelter-in-place rules. I've done my best to keep everybody safe and happy, though."

A Me whizzed by on a zip line that stretched from the trash compactor escape room to the zero-grav acid paintball arena.

"Safe and happy?" said Meticulous, grabbing his neatly folded clothes from a chair outside the shower. "This looks more like desperation."

"Oh, come on." I slipped into the fresh T-shirt and jeans that Prez and his MeMinder had made for me. It felt good to wear regular clothes again, even if they came from a 3-D printer. "Mes would be going stir-crazy cooped up inside without stuff to do."

"You got that right," said Cowboy. "You two galoots notice how none of them Mes back there tried to come to blows with you?"

"Yeah, we didn't have a repeat of the big Me rumble that went down in the Janus," said Juvenile Hall. "Remember that, Cowboy?"

Cowboy didn't miss the edge in Juvenile Hall's voice. "Yeah, hoss, I remember how we had it out. And we can have it again anytime you want!"

"Can it, you two!" said Acupuncture. "We Mes are in a happier space now! So embrace your inner peace. Or else!"

Meticulous stepped out from behind the curtain, tying the cravat of his new colonial-style outfit. "I don't see how deadly thrill rides will help anybody achieve 'inner peace.' And I especially don't see the value of those Me challenges. What's to be gained from flipping a bottle for hours on end?"

"Dance challenges, eating challenges, bucket challenges, all challenges have always been an integral part of life on Earth Zero," said Prez.

"Seriously?" I said. "They're mostly just for laughs where I'm from."

"They entertain us too. But they also inspire us to be our best. They're an indispensable way to connect, spread values, teach important life lessons."

"Quite," said Meticulous. "People are certainly at their best when stuffing their mouths with marshmallows to the point of slobbering."

Prez laughed, although with the slightest hint of annoyance. "Say what you will, but my run for the presidency was helped in no small measure by the exposure I got when I competed in the national Origami Challenge."

"Brilliant, you can fold paper," said Meticulous. "Just what I'm looking for in a leader."

Prez and Meticulous played a game of who-can-fake-smile-the-longest.

"So," I said, if only to break up the tension, "this is definitely a cool setup you've built. But if you got all this stuff from the Rip, how'd you find it and haul it here? I thought the Rip dumped its deposits at random all over the place."

Juvenile Hall lowered his voice like he was letting us in on a big secret. "Dig this. We've managed to exert some control over the Rip."

"Rubbish!" said Meticulous.

"What sort of control?" I asked. "You can just dial up whatever you want?"

"Hardly," said Juvenile Hall. "We've made a connection to the Rip that lets us monitor all the jazz that's coming in and direct it here."

"That's impossible!" said Meticulous. "First of all, you'd need the technology I developed for the origami drive. Then you'd need some kind of probe, plus something to launch it into the Rip."

Juvenile Hall pointed to a missile launcher off in the distance. "Dig that, daddy-o."

Prez nodded. "Refitting that thing to launch our probe is just one of Juvenile Hall's innovations as chief scientist around here."

"Scientist?" I had a hard time tamping down my surprise.

"He's no scientist!" said Meticulous. "He's a dodgy hooligan!"

Juvenile Hall smirked. "You're stereotyping me. Not cool, man. You wanna know why I wound up in juvie? 'Cause I was cooking up an origami drive of my own back on my Earth. Got it close to working too. But then it kinda blew up my lab."

Meticulous sniffed. "I doubt you were *that* close. Nobody smart enough to achieve a level of control over the Rip would use it to build some barmy theme park!"

"Heck, the REAL loot we sock away!" Cowboy said as a roller coaster powered by a booster rocket flew past.

Acupuncture pointed to a building on the edge of the common. It looked like someone had scooped the roof off the White House and dumped the Taj Mahal on top of it.

"I get it now," said Meticulous. "You keep the best doodads for yourself, like the palaces that come your way."

"Not at all," said Prez. "I sleep in a dorm with the other Mes. We use the Taj Ma White House for storage."

"What do you store?" I said.

"Y'all wouldn't believe the geegaws we got stabled in there," said Cowboy. "Renewable-energy generators strong enough to power a city! Water purifiers that can scrub a river clean as a whistle!"

Meticulous eyed the Toga Mes circling around the Taj Ma White House on patrol. "And how many Mes do you have guarding the place?"

Prez laughed. "These things aren't for you to steal for your corporation. They're for everyone to share. They're going to be our gift to every Earth in the multiverse!"

"Gift?" I said. "What are you talking about?"

"I'm not sending the Mes home empty-handed," said Prez. "They'll be taking these wonders with them, to their Earths."

"They'll share these miracles and use them to restore balance and peace to their worlds," said Acupuncture. "And if they don't, we'll knock some sense into them!"

"Seriously, how much do you plan to charge for all this loot?" said Meticulous. "Better be careful about the exchange rates. They use actual bread as currency on Hollywood's Earth. It's a right pain to convert that into pounds."

"That's the coolness of it all, man," said Juvenile. "We won't be charging nothing."

"Way we figure it, all them Earths out there need our help, by gum!" said Cowboy. "And it's our duty to provide it."

Meticulous wagged a finger at Prez. "So that's it! You want to be the one who controls who gets what! You want to be an influencer! The greatest influencer in the multiverse!"

Prez shrugged. "If being an influencer means influencing the gradual improvement of every Earth out there, then call me an influencer."

"But what about when you run out of stuff to hand out?" I said.

"What do you mean, run out?" said Acupuncture. "It's a great big multiverse out there, and it blesses us with its glorious bounty every day. It'd better, or else!"

"Yeah, I don't see this particular water hole drying up," said Cowboy.

"Oh, it'll dry up, all right," said Meticulous. "Once I, with Average as my assistant, fix the Rip once and for all."

"I'm not your assistant!" I said.

Prez and his team looked confused.

"Yo, who said anything about fixing the Rip?" said Juvenile Hall.

"We plan on leaving the Rip open for a long, long time," said Prez. "After all, if it ain't broke, don't nix it."

15

Ripped a New One

Most Mes you could read like a picture book. Prez was more like a top secret file with all the important lines blacked out. He controlled his face so well that I had no idea what was going through his mind as he told us again, in all apparent seriousness, that he actually believed a tear in the fabric of reality was no big deal.

"The Rip is a gateway to other worlds," said Prez. "It's too precious a resource to just throw away. Meticulous, surely you can see the benefit."

Meticulous looked like someone had just told him with a straight face that the world was flat, or that perfect attendance at school was something actually worth celebrating with an award. His disbelief had left him speechless, so I spoke for him. "There won't be any benefit for anybody if the Rip blows up everything."

"You just need to see the same facts we're seeing," said Prez. "Juvenile Hall, would you show them the Rip monitor?"

Juvenile Hall pulled up a screen on his MePad that featured a cartoon of the Rip shooting lightning down on tiny Earths all lined up in a row. Each bolt would strike an Earth, then rebound and hit another Earth nearby. The cycle continued over and over. A smaller screen on the side recorded which Earths got struck, plus lots of other numbers that made no sense to me.

"Now that we got our peepers on the Rip, we don't miss much," said Juvenile Hall. "Dig this: we even saw you cats comin' from Earth Ninety-Nine."

"Wait a minute," I said. "That thing can tell who and what comes through the Rip? Did it record where my family and friends got zapped to?"

Meticulous, still tongue-tied, gave me a grateful nod. And for the first time ever, I felt like we had something in common besides DNA.

Juvenile Hall scrolled through the log of numbers, stopping at an entry just a few hours old. "Solid, man! Here's a reading of several cats getting transferred from your Earth to another, but I can't get a clear fix anywhere. Too much interference at the scene. Still, they made it!"

Like a toilet that's just been unclogged, I felt waves of

relief flow through me. Mom, Dad, Twig, Nash, Lil Battleship, Caveman, and Barbra were all okay. I had no idea where they were or how to get there, but at least they'd survived. And if they'd escaped death, chances seemed better than ever that Motor, Hollywood, Resist, and the Virals had too.

Meticulous looked happy enough to speak again, but him opening his big mouth wasn't necessarily a good thing. "Just because you have some AccuWeather multiverse forecast now, you really think you can control the Rip? It's an unstable menace! It can't be tamed!"

Prez clapped his hands together. "But that's just it: you two have proven the Rip *can* be tamed! You controlled the Rip enough to travel here, didn't you?"

"Hardly!" I said. "We're lucky to be alive!"

"Well, that's a bit of an exaggeration," said Meticulous. "I knew what I was doing when I brought us here. But in general, sure, I agree with Average for once. The Rip is much too dangerous for anyone else to mess with. It has to be shut down."

"Maybe I can change your tune," said Prez.

He nodded to Acupuncture, who pulled a car key fob from his pocket and clicked it. A garage door on the side of the Taj Ma White House opened, and a blue convertible limo flew out, gliding on a cushion of air.

"Yep, we got us a hover limo," said Cowboy.

Meticulous made a fart noise with his lips. "I came across hover tech like this years ago but found it too dangerous to use."

94

"Jump back, Jack!" said Juvenile Hall. "You mean to tell me you found a gizmo and didn't steal it?"

"Ha ha, you're brilliant," muttered Meticulous.

Acupuncture pressed the fob again, and the limo's doors popped open.

"Hop in," said Prez. He pointed toward a wide canyon just outside the boundary of Me HQ. "Let's take a tour of the junkyard of the multiverse."

16

Heap of Fun

Big Ben with a giant digital clock display blinking twelve o'clock over and over. A bagpipe-playing robot blaring the *Jurassic Park* theme song on a loop. A family minivan decked out with spiked wheels, missile launchers, and a back-seat gun battery.

As Acupuncture flew the hover limo into the canyon, I couldn't wrap my head around the sheer amount of stuff the Rip had dumped there. Endless rows of alternate-Earth buildings, vehicles, furniture, and other random garbage lined the ledges and filled alcoves dug into the dirt walls.

Meticulous seemed unconcerned about all this strangeness as he scrolled through the limo's built-in monitor, skimming through memes and other clips. I figured he must have been desperate for screen time after being stranded with no electronics for so long. That had been my fault, like so many other things.

With Prez and Cowboy distracted by an avalanche of cinnamon rolls the size of beanbag chairs, I whispered to Juvenile Hall in the seat beside me. "Tell me something. How do you . . . move on after being locked up?"

"Move on?" asked Juvenile Hall. "Whoa, man, that's a crazy scene to think about. I've still got more of my sentence to serve when I get back. Probably longer, now that I've been gone so long. They must think I ran away. But listen, bad is as bad does, you feel me? Don't let that place do a number on your head. You're more than just a kid in juvie."

"Thanks for saying that. And I also wanted to say it's really cool of you not to get mad at me for ditching everybody at Me Con."

"Aw, it's nothing," said Juvenile Hall. "It ain't like any of that was your fault, man. You got detained, that's all."

I appreciated the words, but I still felt like an all-around louse.

We passed a ledge stuffed with an entire living room furniture set covered in disco ball mirrors. "So why does so much stuff from the Rip come to this spot, anyway?" I asked.

"Because of that." Meticulous pointed to a big steel dome at the bottom of the canyon. I'd been too lost in my thoughts to notice we were flying straight for it. "Whatever's under that is drawing the Rip like a magnet," he added.

Prez raised his hands in mock surrender. "Right again. How *do* you do it?" He nodded to Juvenile Hall, who tapped a button on his MePad. The dome swung open, knocking aside a couple of copies of famous statues: *David* carrying a skateboard and Ronald McDonald as *The Thinker*. Underneath sat a huge ring of steel mounted on a platform like a satellite dish.

At the sight of it, Meticulous and I jinxed each other again: "You built a giant origami drive?!"

The machine looked almost exactly like the engine Meticulous had used to power dimension-hopping elevators, just blown up ten times as big.

Meticulous squinted at the ring. "It's not finished."

"Right," I said. "Because if it were complete, it could make portals to other Earths like the original."

Meticulous scowled at me. "I was supposed to say that!"

Prez laughed. "Oh, you two! But you're right, it's a work in progress. This origami drive lets us harvest the Rip but not control it. But now, with your help, we can change that."

Acupuncture circled the platform, looking for a place to land.

"Origami drives are dangerous, and I'm through with them," said Meticulous. "We need to focus on fixing the Rip, not exploiting it. Look how much worse it's gotten since you opened that dome!"

Meticulous pointed to the sky. The Rip had grown darker, crackling with lightning again. "Your experiments are tearing the Rip apart even faster than if you'd left it alone! You're making it worse!"

"No, we're making it better," said Prez. "The drive keeps most of the Rip's storms focused on this spot, which spares the rest of Earth Zero the worst of it. Now the bulk of the random stuff ends up here instead."

"Then why is the Rip dropping deserts and maple syrup lakes all over the place?" I said.

"And why is the Rip going all to pot on other Earths too?!" said Meticulous. It was a relief to be arguing on his side and not against him for once.

A bolt shot down from the Rip and struck the drive. The ring filled with a familiar field of green energy, the stuff I called transdimensional goop. Another bolt blasted the platform, missing the drive by inches. It left behind a rawhide dog chew toy in the shape of a full-size human.

With no warning, Acupuncture spun around in the driver seat and hurled needles at Meticulous and me. Once the points dug into our shoulders, we couldn't move a muscle between us.

As Acupuncture flew the limo directly over the origami drive, Prez reached across Meticulous and popped open the door by his side. "Wish it didn't have to be like this, but our timetable's been pushed up, and we don't have a second left to convince you."

Juvenile Hall pulled down his shades to look me straight in the eyes. "Sorry, daddy-o."

He and Prez scooted out of the way so Cowboy could grab Meticulous and me by the arms and toss us out the door.

We dropped until we smacked into the field of green goop. It caught us like a circus trapeze net, springy but solid. Hanging there felt like being stuck in the moment when your chair tips back too far and you have no idea whether or not you've reached the point of no return.

From the limo above, Cowboy lassoed some sort of power cable to an antenna on the drive. Juvenile Hall plugged the other end of the cable into a MeMinder charging pad.

Movement trickled back into my muscles, but as I squirmed to get free, the goop bounced right along with me, never letting go. It was like I'd been woven into a trampoline. It didn't help that Meticulous thrashed around too, bouncing us even more. For a second there I worried we might get thrown off the thing, but we seemed thoroughly stuck.

"Stop it already!" I shouted.

Meticulous growled a series of British curse words and went still. Even so, it took forever for us to stop shaking. There wasn't much to do but watch Prez in the limo up above as he placed his MeMinder in the charging cradle.

"What gives?" I called to him. "What are you doing?"

"Isn't it obvious?" said Meticulous. "He's leeching your power. He's taking away your precious fizz so he can access it through his MeMinder."

Prez beamed at us, and even after what he'd just done, I still couldn't deny how charming he was. "Well done figuring that out! Again, I'm sorry to inconvenience you like this, but you two are the secret ingredient we've been missing. The ability you both share to fizz is quite a gift. Now it's time to share that gift with the rest of us!"

"What are you on about?" said Meticulous. "I may be exceptional, but I don't *fizz*. I don't rely on any special powers!"

"Not according to our readings, man," said Juvenile Hall. He held up his MePad, which showed a picture of Meticulous surrounded by an aura of light. "The origami drive scanned you, and it don't lie, Jack. It shows you can fizz, just like we figured. You can't do it as much as Average, but you still got the goods."

In a huff, Meticulous stomped his foot, making the web of goop quake worse than a bouncy house at a five-year-old's birthday party. "Average got those powers at birth!" he whined. "From his mum trying to open portals while he was in the womb! That never happened to any other Me!"

"You've done a lot of experiments with portals too," Acupuncture said from the driver's seat. "Maybe you were affected by all that like Average."

"Whatever the case," said Prez, "there's no denying you've got the fizz."

Cowboy tugged on the cable to make sure it was secure. "Ain't it funny, Meticulous? You done bragged about how you could master any skill, but all along you were just cheating with superpowers, like Average."

"Now, now," said Prez. "Let's remember that we're all Mes here. So, shall we get this dough on the road?"

101

Juvenile Hall pressed a button on his MePad, and lightning crackled through the goop holding us up. Pinpricks jabbed every cell in my body, and then my insides lit on fire. I thought I heard Meticulous scream, but it could just as easily have been me. We screamed alike, after all.

For a moment, the fizz flared in me stronger than ever. My body could have broken free in a dozen ways. My mind could have dreamed up a hundred escape plans. But just like that, the feeling of invincibility shrank to nothing, leaving a cave in my guts.

It was over. I wasn't All of Me anymore. I was just Average. Just a nobody. Just another Me.

17

Fizzed Out

Meticulous and I hung in the origami drive's energy field like two bugs sucked dry in a web. "I don't get it," said Meticulous. "I never had the fizz. So why do I feel so knackered?"

Knackered. That was one way to describe the feeling of having your superpowers vacuumed straight out of your body.

Up above, sparks ran along the cable to the charger on the limo, bathing Prez's MeMinder in a green glow. Getting the go-ahead from Juvenile Hall, Prez pried the MeMinder from its perch and strapped it to his wrist. He jumped as a flash of green burst from the watch, then laughed when he realized it didn't hurt. He tapped at the screen and summoned a sheet of holo-paper. Within seconds, he'd folded it into an animal shape.

The barest trickle of fizz dripped into my brain, telling me what he'd just folded. "Long-wattled umbrella bird," I said to Meticulous. "Earth One Hundred Twenty-Five."

"So your fizz isn't completely gone after all," he said. "Good. You'll need it."

Just like the portal paper, the bird origami ballooned into a doorway between Earths. The other Mes in the limo went silent as Prez stepped through it, disappearing from our universe like he'd never been there at all. After a few moments, he came back, a triumphant smile on his face. "We've got control of the Rip! Mes, this is your ticket home!"

Cowboy yee-hawed as the Mes high-fived each other.

Prez looked down on us with a big thumbs-up. "You two have done a great job, and I'm sorry again that we had to do it this way. We want to run a few more tests before we get you out, so just hang in there a little longer. We'll get back to you in a sniffy."

"You mean 'in a jiffy,' you prat!" Meticulous yelled up to him. But the limo had already flown out of hearing range.

"I don't get it," I said. "Why did they need to steal our fizz to do this?"

Meticulous kept his eyes fixed on the limo, like it might do something any second. "What do you mean, *our* fizz?"

"Admit it. You being able to fizz explains a lot."

Meticulous tore his eyes from the limo to glare at me. "And just what do you mean by that?!"

"For starters, how you're way too competent at everything," I said. "It makes sense that you've had a boost all this time."

"I've trained hard all my life to get the skills I have! I'm not some cheater like you. Or like Prez!"

"I still don't even understand what Prez has done."

Meticulous shook his head. "So much potential, wasted on an inferior brain. With your fizz powering his advanced MeMinder, Prez is basically wearing a fully functioning origami drive on his wrist. That makes him the most powerful person in the multiverse."

As that sank in, Meticulous looked back up to the limo. "Anytime now," he muttered.

"What are you talking about?"

"You didn't think I'd let myself become a prisoner without a backup plan, did you?"

The limo shot upward as if yanked by a bungee cord.

"Yes!" said Meticulous.

"You did that?" The answer to my own question hit me. "You hacked the limo when you were pretending to watch memes!"

Meticulous yawned. "I simply made a few suggestions to the navigation system."

"So would you say you were fizzing the hacking skills of Troll Me or Motor Me?"

"I wasn't *fizzing* anyone but me! And by the way, brace yourself."

Before I could ask what he meant, the energy field in the origami drive snuffed out and we both fell butt-first down to the platform below.

"You knew the drive would turn off?" I said, getting to my feet.

"Juvenile Hall's controls are out of range," he said.

"You really planned this to the letter."

"Naturally," he said, dusting himself off. "I'm meticulous."

"So what's the next part of your plan?" I said.

"Isn't it obvious?" said Meticulous. "You've got a sheet of portal paper ready to go."

"No I don't. Your portal paper got trashed."

"I didn't say *my* portal paper," he said. "Look at your trousers."

The front pocket of my jeans glowed. Once I got over the shock of wearing a pair of radioactive pants, I remembered how I'd shoved the unfolded ouroboros there when I changed clothes. I pried the pocket open with a finger, and green light shot out, practically burning my eyes.

"That note was written on portal paper," he said. "The origami drive must have charged it up."

After reaching into my pocket with the slow and steady hand of a bomb defuser, I teased the crumpled paper into the open air. Meticulous held out his hand like he expected me to give it to him. I pretended not to notice as I smoothed out the wrinkles.

"Hand it over," said Meticulous. "I'll fold the portal to Earth One."

I took a step back. "I'm not going to Earth One!"

"*I'm* not going to unicorn world!"

"Well, *I* have to find my friends!"

"*I* have to find my equipment!" he said.

Just then, the limo stopped in midair, wobbled for a moment, and pointed downward to fly straight at us. "Come on, guys!" Prez shouted through the limo's speakers. "Let's talk this out!"

Meticulous gave the oncoming car what I figured must have been Earth One's rudest hand gesture. With him distracted, I started speed-folding the paper into a unicorn. It wasn't my finest work, especially once Meticulous got wise to me and tried to snatch the paper away. From that point on, I had to fold while playing keep-away from him.

I'd managed to finish most of the body and had just started on the horn when Meticulous got a solid grip on the unicorn butt. Holding its horn, I pulled harder than I should have and the paper ripped in half.

Green energy flew everywhere, knocking us backward. But here's the weirdest part: we never landed. Instead of hitting the ground, we kept falling through whatever trapdoor the blast had opened in the multiverse.

Where we'd end up was anybody's guess.

18

Try to Trick Me

Kentucky Fried Griffon cooks the choicest cuts of breasts, legs, and wings with a blend of seven secret herbs and spices to produce a magical taste sensation that's finger-claw-and-hoof-lickin' good.

Or so I learned from the tiny winged fairy shouting a sales pitch outside the fast-food joint.

On my Earth, a Kentucky Fried Chicken stood on this spot. On Earth One, it was a British-ified Kentucky Fried Fish and Chips. But neither of those versions featured a little person with butterfly wings hawking the menu in a screechy voice.

I had an ongoing debate with Mom and Dad about how

Frodo Baggins, Conan the Barbarian, and other characters from medieval-fantasy books and movies would get by in the modern world. The Earth where the portal paper had sent us was a case study in that very question. And then some.

Magic was real here, but it had kept up with the times. Along the cobblestone streets of downtown, a bearded wizard bought cross-trainers from an elf cobbler. A family of ogres hauled a squeaky wooden cart filled with back-to-school-sale deals. A genie picked up a three-headed orange tabby cat from a grooming salon. A bunch of panting Minotaurs in Camp Gladiator shirts ordered smoothies at a juice stand. It was as if a bunch of characters in a *Dungeons & Dragons* adventure had bailed on their quest and gone shopping.

All these beings had embraced another important part of modern life: screen addiction. They carried crystal balls and wouldn't stop looking at them as they messaged people, checked social media, took selfies, and watched viral visions. The glass spheres kept them so distracted that no one seemed to notice how Meticulous and I looked alike. They seemed just as oblivious to the Rip overhead. The hole in the multiverse was calmer on this Earth, but still hard to miss. Maybe in a world where packs of flying monkeys flew overhead on a regular basis, a glowing green tear in the sky was no big deal.

Meticulous refused to take in any of these sights and sounds. Since we'd arrived, he'd just been sitting on the curb beside me, cradling his head in his hands (though careful not to muss his hair). "Magic can't be real," he kept muttering to himself. "It can't be!"

"Maybe it's super-science," I said as a pack of fish people walked by with yoga mats rolled up under their shoulders.

"My entire worldview has been shattered!" said Meticulous. "Why did you drag us here?"

In the distance, construction worker giants in hard hats put together a new skyscraper as if they were playing Legos. "I have a feeling Motor and the others are here," I said. "Maybe None of Me sent the note. Maybe he's some sort of dark wizard after all, and this is his Earth. He's probably captured them. Maybe he's been pumping them for info on you and me."

Meticulous dodged a hunk of Pegasus poop that dropped from overhead. "If that's the case, then you chose to fall into a completely obvious trap. And all for the sake of a hunch rather than listening to me! You could have taken me to Earth One, where I have work to finish!"

"Things were down to the wire! I hadn't even finished folding the origami key before you got all grabby!"

"Need I remind you that you're the one who ripped the portal paper? It's a bloody miracle we even made it here. Our one chance to get to my Earth and you blew it!"

"I don't even see the point of going to Earth One if you haven't finished this Stitch thing. If it's even real."

"The Stitch is very much real! And it certainly won't get finished while we're wasting our time here!" He waved his hands at a teenage vampire operating a sno-cone stand across the street, like she'd done something wrong.

"You expect too much out of Mes!" I said. "We can't all be perfect like you!"

"For once you've said something that makes sense!" said Meticulous.

All of a sudden, a glowing green *M* sliced open the air between us. It wasn't just any *M* either.

"The Me Corp. logo?" said Meticulous.

The *M* expanded into a portal and a fairy flew through it. He carried a shiny new crystal ball in a clear case emblazoned with another stylized *M*. Ignoring us, the fairy flapped the package over to a shop called Potion Notions across the street.

Slack-jawed with the same exact amount of slack, Meticulous and I watched the portal disappear into nothing.

"There's a Me Corp. here?" I said.

Meticulous poked at the residue of green energy still clinging to the air. "And it looks like they use some of the most advanced magic around. I'd expect no less from the Me Corp. brand."

"If Me Corp. can make portals to deliver stuff, maybe they can make a portal to get us to Earth One!" I said.

Meticulous pointed to a tower that rose above everything else on the skyline. Massive thorn-encrusted vines covered the building from top to bottom, as if the giant in "Jack and the Beanstalk" worked a nine-to-five office job there.

"That's got to be Me Corp.," he said. "Me Corps. on every

Earth are always in the tallest buildings in any given skyline."

"I wonder how it got Sleeping Beautied," I said.

"What are you on about?" asked Meticulous.

"You know, the curse in 'Sleeping Beauty'? The evil fairy makes a barrier of plants to keep out the prince?"

Meticulous got to his feet. "My Earth's version of 'Sleeping Beauty' involves the princess falling asleep after pulling an all-nighter to prep for her medical school entrance exam the next day. She winds up rescuing herself and acing the test."

We headed for the tower, nobody giving either of us a second glance. On the way, we passed a display of crystal balls in a Me Corp. shop window. They all showed a familiar face: Me. Or rather, a heroic, fantasy Me. He wore chain mail with a sword on his side and thick metal boots and gloves. When I leaned in for a closer look, a vision bloomed inside my head. It played out like the opening-credits montage of a TV show, images of the Me sharpening his sword, strapping on armor, and talking his way out of a traffic ticket from a hobbit cop.

Meticulous slapped his forehead. "Get out of my brain! Haven't they heard of privacy laws here?!"

A narrator spoke. "You're experiencing a vision of *The Chosen One,* everyone's favorite reality show. Tonight, an episode like none other. Two days ago, the Chosen One was seen entering Me Corp. Tower, the home and office of the company's CEO, that mysterious billionaire, the Dark Lord himself."

The vision showed a mug shot of None of Me, the familiar hood covering his face. Then it switched back to the Warrior Me marching up to the thorn-covered tower.

"Hold up," I said. "How are there two Mes here?"

"Shush!" said Meticulous. "Talking during a show is punishable with jail time on most Earths."

"Though consumers' love of Me Corp. products hasn't slackened," the announcer continued, "many have questioned the Dark Lord's connection to the dangerous green storms originating from the tear that has appeared over our skies. Unconfirmed reports have also circulated that Me Corp. may be deliberately cursing its products. Refusing comment, the Dark Lord has locked himself away in Me Corp. Tower. Now his brother, the Chosen One, has set out to find answers. As the two prepare to face off in an epic family battle, the world waits, breathless to see which of them survives."

"His brother?!" I said.

Meticulous patted his eyebrows. "Me twins. That's new."

The vision switched to a commercial break, and yet another Me appeared in my mind: Motor Me. I couldn't believe it. My long-lost friend looked very much alive as he sat at an old wooden table surrounded by books and flasks full of bubbling potions. With an awkward smile, Motor raised his hand and shot a miniature display of fireworks from his fingers. Then he sang a jingle. In rhyme:

"Polymagic Vocational Institute.
It's magic! It's practical! And it's a real
    hoot!"

The image freeze-framed on Motor giving the camera the same painful grin I reserved for pictures and videos I didn't want to be in.

An announcer's voice took over:

"Classes available starting today.
Practical magic just a few blocks away!
Take Magic Forest Freeway and exit Mount Dread.
A few steps from there and you'll reach our homestead!"

The vision cleared.

Meticulous shook his head. "This better not be one of those Earths where everybody rhymes when they talk! The only thing mankier than that are Earths where they only speak pig Latin!"

"The candy bar wrappers weren't a fluke!" I said. "He's here after all! And maybe the others too! We've gotta go to that school."

"I suppose he may have information to help us get off this rubbish Earth." Meticulous nodded. "I will allow this."

"Thanks, Your Majesty. I'm so grateful."

Not even Meticulous's attitude could get to me now. I was about to get my best friend back.

But first, I had to break into a magic school.

19

Magic in Me

When we'd set off for a real-life magic school, I'd been expecting something as magnificent as Hogwarts Castle or as mysterious as Doctor Strange's Sanctum Sanctorum. But the multiverse let me down yet again: the Polymagic Vocational Institute turned out to be housed in the same old stupid County Youth Development building on my Earth, and Me HQ on Earth Zero. Would I never get away from this place?

"Sure, it's feeling a little repetitive," said Meticulous, leading me across the common yard to a small window on the rear wall. "But I noticed that the lock on this bathroom window was dodgy on both Earth Ninety-Nine and Earth Zero."

"How would you notice something like that?!" I asked.

"I'm meticulous. And I'd be willing to bet the lock is compromised on this Earth too."

He bonked his fist on the latch, and the window popped open.

"This is not a good deed!" warned the MeMinder X as we climbed into the school.

We tiptoed across the room and opened the door. I held out hope that the school might be magically bigger on the inside than it looked on the outside. No such luck. Even with class in session and no students around, the main hallway felt more cramped than the one at Youth Development back home. The walls were stacked to capacity with racks of filthy potion flasks, stinky cauldrons, piles of mud-drenched flying carpets, and streaky magic mirrors.

"It's like a flea market for down-and-out wizards," said Meticulous as we stepped out of the bathroom.

I almost laughed, until I reminded myself that I wasn't supposed to enjoy Meticulous's jokes.

A pair of giant floating lips appeared out of thin air and shushed us. Startled, I bumped into a passing cart full of swords sticking out of large stones. The goblin pushing the cart smirked at me and pointed to a sign on the wall as he moved along. FINAL EXAM DAY, read the sign. QUIET, PLEASE!

"This is good," whispered Meticulous. "Everyone will be so anxious about their tests, they won't pay us any mind."

As the goblin moved on, one of the stones fell off his cart. It looked like a huge hunk of coal, with a knife just as dark sticking out of it. Having been forced by Mom and Dad to watch every King Arthur movie and TV show ever, I couldn't resist giving the hilt a hard pull. The last thing I expected was for it to slide right out. I gazed at the knife in my hand, marveling at how the dark blade seemed to suck up all the light around it. It was like a shadow that wouldn't go away.

"This is not a good deed," said the MeMinder X.

"What a weird knife," I said, running my finger along the dull edge. It needed a good sharpening.

Meticulous shrugged. "Keep it. Could come in handy. Now come on."

Like Meticulous figured, the final exams kept the students and teachers so focused that nobody noticed Meticulous or me and the fact that we weren't wearing denim wizard robes like everybody else.

We kept mum as we passed classroom after classroom, looking for Motor in each. We saw plenty of humans, elves, dwarves, talking forest creatures, bird people, and even a talking candelabra. But no Motor.

For a magic school, this place wasn't so magical. These students weren't training to become wizards. They were settling for making and repairing the things that wizards used. They whittled staffs, welded cauldrons, wove flying carpets, and sewed invisibility cloaks with unseen needles and thread.

Meticulous grimaced at the sight of a wand-polishing test in progress as we walked along. "This place may as well just be a glorified shop class for role-playing-game enthusiasts."

"Would you shut up already?" I said as we ran into a stretch of hallway blocked off by a Do Not Cross tape barrier. An indoor blizzard raged on the other side.

"That's magic for you," said Meticulous. "Guess we'll have to backtrack."

Just as we turned around, a pair of hands shoved me against a wall. Eardrum held me in place, and Slime stood at his side. They both wore denim wizard robes, which meant they must have been the local version of my least favorite kids on any Earth.

Meticulous lurked behind them, too busy chuckling to himself to actually lift a finger and help.

"Look at Macon, getting around on his own two feet," said Eardrum. "Why aren't you at Magical Cleaning right now for the exam?"

"Yeah, and what happened to your uniform?" asked Slime.

"Doesn't matter." Eardrum aimed a fist at my face, like the other two versions of him had done on every other Earth I'd visited. "You're about to get a failing grade anyway."

I guess Meticulous figured he'd left me hanging long enough. He stepped behind Eardrum and clamped a hand on his shoulder. "Oh please, couldn't you have come up with a better line?!" And with that, he squeezed.

Nothing happened.

Meticulous looked from his hand to Eardrum. Then the

awareness sank in—he might have practiced Acupuncture's nerve pinch over and over, but without the fizz, he couldn't pull it off. All this time, he'd been relying on superpowers more than he'd known.

I might have enjoyed the sight of Meticulous actually failing for once, but this wasn't the time to be petty. With Eardrum and Slime occupied, I pulled the black knife from my belt and waved it in the air, hoping to scare them. The dull and dinky little blade shook in my hands, and a creepy chorus of chanting monks blasted from the hilt. Everybody watched as the weapon grew into a full-length sword, thick and sharp and covered in nasty-looking runes.

Eardrum and Slime backed away.

"The Shadow Blade!" Slime cried.

"'Only the darkest of hearts shall wield the darkest of blades,'" said Eardrum. I imagined he was quoting some sort of sinister poem, but I'd only ever heard him quote especially stupid memes, so I couldn't be sure.

The sword lit up with black flames running from its hilt to its tip like some sort of negative torch. I would have thrown the thing to the floor, but the dancing shadows mesmerized me. The sword had an even stronger effect on everybody else. Eardrum and Slime passed out cold, and Meticulous got so woozy, he had to lean against the wall.

Then, with no warning, the Shadow Blade puffed into a cloud of ash that hung in the air like smog before drifting away.

I shuddered. "What just happened?"

Meticulous wiped his hands together like he'd taken out the goons by himself. "Oh, it's just some magical silliness. Don't get all whingey about it." He eyed Eardrum's uniform. "Who thought up these outfits? No fashion sense! But they'll help us fit in."

Meticulous yanked the robe off Eardrum, leaving him on the floor in nothing but boxers decorated with cute little baby dragons. He gestured for me to do the same with Slime.

"Eardrum made it sound like that knife-sword thing was evil," I said, crouching beside Slime and tugging at his outfit. "And that it could only be used by evil people."

"They were being superstitious. Remember: it's just silly magic." Meticulous spotted something in one of Eardrum's pockets and reached inside to pull out a cloth bag of glowing dust. Poof Powder, it read on the side. He scooped a pinch, gave it a closer look, and then flicked the specks off his fingers. They erupted into a miniature mushroom cloud of multicolored smoke.

When the smoke had cleared and we'd finished coughing, Meticulous cinched the drawstrings of the bag and put it in his pocket. "Clearly, they were up to no good, roaming the halls with this stuff. I'll be doing the school a favor by confiscating it."

I tugged Slime's robe over my head. "They said something about Magical Cleaning?"

121

"Sounds like we can find Motor there. Let's go."

After shoving Eardrum and Slime into a supply closet full of cursed jewelry and Cyclops skulls, we headed down the hall in our liberated robes. The whole time, the words Eardrum had recited to me wouldn't leave my brain: *Only the darkest of hearts shall wield the darkest of blades.*

Did that make me evil somehow? I'd always thought people who drew swords out of stones were supposed to be the good guys.

In this case, maybe not so much.

20

Finals Fantasy

A chalkboard floated over the stage in the auditorium: MAGICAL CLEANING FINALS. Students squatted on the floor, cleaning pentacles smudged with blood, candle wax, fur, bits of horns, and brown and yellow stains I didn't want to think about.

We spotted Motor in the back, floating on a magic carpet.

The rug was gray and shaggy, just like the one in Dad's home lab in the basement. I almost got a little choked up at the sight of it—Motor's version of Dad had died, so he must have picked this carpet as some kind of tribute.

Motor whistled a tune as he scrubbed away at his mess. He looked far behind the rest of the class, but at the same time, the least stressed. He hardly seemed to have a care in the world.

"Looks like he's lost a little weight," said Meticulous.

Motor had slimmed down for sure, and he wasn't stress eating either. He didn't even touch the bag of Kraken Crackers in the cup holder attached to the side of his carpet.

From a table at the edge of the stage, wizard versions of Lunt, O'Fartly, and Pooplaski eyed the class like they were desperate for somebody to mess up.

"You have twenty minutes," Lunt told the class. "That should be adequate time to finish the test. Except for Flying Carpet in the back. He's so far behind, there's no hope for him!"

Everyone laughed, and Motor's peppy mood disappeared, replaced by the more familiar crushed and defeated look I remembered him wearing.

"How dare Lunt say that!" said Meticulous. "And Motor just took it like a mummy's boy!"

"Since when are you concerned about Motor?" I said.

"It's not about him," said Meticulous. "It's about anybody thinking they can walk all over a Me. Any Me."

"You're just looking for a fight because you're still angry over getting shown up by Prez. You don't like meeting a Me who's better than you."

Meticulous straightened the sleeves of his uniform. "Better than me? Hardly! Now, we've got to help Motor. Maybe you can find another evil magic sword to wave at them."

Over in his corner, Motor looked so flustered he couldn't even keep a grip on his cleaning brush.

"Nah," I said. "I've got a better idea."

Lunt had just announced fifteen minutes until the end of the test, when a multicolored mushroom cloud appeared on the stage. By the time the screaming died down and the smoke mostly cleared, Meticulous and I had taken spots on either side of Motor.

My friend looked so surprised to see us that he almost fell off his carpet.

"What's the meaning of this!" spluttered Lunt, pointing a spray bottle full of bubbling blue potion at my face. O'Fartly and Pooplaski shook mops at us that glowed with mystical power.

I whispered into Motor's ear: "Tell them we're magical cleaning assistants you've summoned."

It took a few moments, but the words finally sank into Motor's brain.

"Uh," said Motor. "I've summoned some, uh, cleaning clones to assist me."

"Cleaning clones?!" said Lunt.

"That's powerful magic!" said O'Fartly.

"Way beyond your level!" said Pooplaski.

"But is it against the rules?" asked Meticulous. He held up a scroll we'd found in the pocket of Slime's robes. "There's nothing in the school guidebook forbidding magical assistants on exams."

Lunt pulled reams of scrolls out of a bag too small to fit them all. "Get back to work, everybody! We'll sort out this mess!"

The teachers dug through the scrolls as the students returned to the test. Once things settled down, Motor, Meticulous, and I huddled together over the dirty pentacle.

Before we could say anything, Motor reached for an animated broom in the corner and swung it at Meticulous, missing him by several inches. The broom person wiggled their arms and legs like a captured bug.

Meticulous and I burst out laughing. Motor looked confused and hurt. I would have felt the same if my best friend had been laughing at me with everybody's least favorite Me. This was starting to feel like that time Mom accidentally invited a bunch of kids from school who hated each other to my birthday party.

"I don't know what kind of mind control you're using on Average," Motor told Meticulous. "But you'd better stop now!"

Meticulous and I shared a look. "This is going to take some explaining," we said at the same time.

21

Origamagic

After assuring Motor that we weren't laughing at him, just at the magical broom person, I gave him a quick rundown of the past few hours. I skimmed through my time in juvie, the visit from Meticulous, the dangerous growth of the Rip, Prez and his plans, our escape here, and our hope that None of Me might have some answers. I would have gone on, but Meticulous butted in. "Excuse me, but can I borrow that brush?" he asked Motor. "This mess is a travesty!"

Motor scowled at Meticulous. "Why're you so concerned about my final?"

Meticulous snatched the brush from him and started

rubbing it on the floor. "You've been doing it wrong. You need to wipe *with* the grain. Like this."

Some magic in the brush made the bristles spin like miniature tornadoes. As a big swath of gunk came off the floor, Meticulous smiled to himself. Then he saw us staring.

"What?" he said. "I hate magic. But you know what I hate more? A messy floor." He got back to his cleaning.

Of all the Mes, I knew Motor the best, and we could say a lot to each other without words. That's how, just by trading a couple of eye rolls and a *meh* face, we agreed that while we couldn't trust Meticulous, we had to work with him for the chance to fix the Rip once and for all.

With a nod to seal the deal, Motor switched back to verbal mode. "So how did you know to find me here, anyway?"

"The commercial," I said. "We saw it on one of those crystal ball thingies."

Motor made a barf face. "I'm still trying to live that down. Hard enough being the worst student at this place. Now I'm the mascot!"

"Worst student?" said Meticulous, still scrubbing away. "Why'd they pick you for the commercial, then?"

"I'm just about the only kid here who doesn't have some injury from a magical accident," said Motor. "Extra eyes, talons for hands, perpetual-flame hair. Don't get me wrong: I've bungled plenty of magic. I just can't do anything strong enough to cause major damage like that."

"Well, why should you worry?" said Meticulous, watching

129

the kid two pentacles down summon a cloud of hyperactive bubbles with eyes and mouths that sang jingles about cleaning. "I mean, you're just cooling your heels here, right? Hiding out? Keeping an eye on None of Me's tower?"

Motor's face went pink. "Well, the thing is, I've always wanted to be a wizard."

"Who hasn't?" I said.

Meticulous raised his hand. "No interest. Never."

"Okay, not counting Mr. Was-Never-a-Kid," I said.

"No, for real," said Motor. "Remember that experiment I told you about? The one where Dad, uh, died? The thing we were experimenting on was magic. You know, to see if it really existed. And, well, we discovered it all right. Dad died in the accident, so I swore off magic from that point on. That is, until the elevator exploded and dumped us on this Earth. I figure learning magic is kind of like a way to honor him, you know?"

Meticulous stopped brushing and stared at Motor, speechless.

"What's the snarky thing you have to say *this* time?" said Motor.

Meticulous looked hurt. "Why, nothing. It's just—losing a parent isn't easy."

A little stunned, Motor nodded. His eyes got wet.

I felt like a jerk. All those weeks I'd been obsessing about Mom and Dad divorcing while I was locked up, thinking I had it worse than any other Me. I'd completely forgotten that some Mes out there, Mes I knew well, had lost their version of Mom or Dad for good. Divorced parents were better than dead parents any day.

"So where are Hollywood and Resist?" I needed to change the subject before we all started bawling. "Are they taking a different class right now?"

Motor snapped out of his daze. "What are you talking about? They've never enrolled here."

Meticulous shook a cramp out of his scrubbing hand. "Of course. Hollywood would sooner die than go to school. Even a fake school like this. And Resist would find magic a waste of time."

"When did he get so good at reading Mes?" said Motor.

"Tell me about it," I grumbled.

"I haven't seen Resist in months," said Motor. "She's disappeared. I figure she's trying to stir up some kind of big protest movement, unionize the delivery fairies or something. As for Hollywood, everybody in the United Republic of Xanadu has been keeping up with him. All you need is a crystal ball."

I put two and two together. "The *Chosen One* show?! That's Hollywood?! They said he was None of Me's twin!"

"Nah, they just made up the brother-against-brother thing for ratings," said Motor.

"I knew it was a fake," said Meticulous, finishing the top point of the pentacle. It looked a lot cleaner than the rest.

"It's real enough," said Motor. "It may be a phony reality

show, but Hollywood really has to confront this Dark Lord. It's in his contract. And he's out of options for putting it off."

"What do you mean, putting it off?" I asked.

"He's avoided going to None of Me's tower for weeks," said Motor. "He spent multiple episodes shopping for just the right weapons and armor and interviewing potential sidekicks to bring along. There was a whole arc of episodes called 'Makeover Quest,' where he tried out different hairstyles."

Meticulous groaned. "Sounds like Hollywood all right."

I felt bummed all of a sudden, and before I could even sort out why, Motor asked me, "Are you okay?" Even by Me standards we were super in tune with each other.

I tried to smile, but couldn't fake it. "I don't know. I guess I was hoping a Me out there might really be an honest-to-goodness Chosen One."

Meticulous flung extra suds off the brush. "Chosen One, Dark Lord, good, bad, it's all the same. All that matters is whether or not None of Me can get us to Earth One, so I can get the Stitch up and running."

Motor shivered. "So you think None of Me could help us?"

"We need to get into his tower and find out," I said. "Any ideas how to get in?"

"Well, I found a clue," said Motor. "I just don't understand it yet."

"I'm sure that won't be a problem for me," said Meticulous, moving on to a new arm of the pentacle. "Just hand it over and I'll figure it out."

Motor glanced at Lunt, Pooplaski, and O'Fartly, who snapped their eyes back to their scrolls, like they hadn't been spying on us. He dropped his voice to a whisper. "It's something None of Me wrote, when he went to school here."

"He went to school here?!" said Meticulous.

"You don't remind anybody of him?" I asked Motor.

"Oh, hardly anybody's seen him with his hood off," said Motor. "And I told the administrators I'm a distant cousin named Macadamia Macon. Don't look at me like that, guys. It was the first name that popped into my head!"

"So why'd he go to this dump?" asked Meticulous.

"Ignore him—" I started.

"Actually, that's fair," said Motor. "The truth is, this used to be the premier magic school of the land, and None of Me was *the* top student. So good, in fact, that he taught some of the classes. But after he left to start his own company, the other talented students left too, including the Twig and Nash of this Earth. Then there were budget cuts, and pretty soon the place had to give up on cool magic and stick with all this boring practical magic."

Meticulous waved his brush in the air. "Hence, a master class in magical cleaning."

"This place is barely keeping afloat," Motor said. "In fact, if we don't win the big game tonight, we'll lose a key athletics grant that's a huge part of the budget. The whole school could shut down. And as a very reluctant member of the team, I can assure you: we don't stand a chance. After we lose, which we're certain to do, the school could close its doors for good."

"I'm starting to find all this dead boring," said Meticulous. He watched a nearby student order the ghost of an anteater to deep-clean the splattered bugs on her pentacle. "Can we get back to the clue None of Me left?"

"You have two minutes left to finish the test!" Lunt screamed before returning to the scrolls. With the clock about to run down, he and the other teachers seemed more desperate than ever to find something in their rules to bust us.

"Sorry!" I told Motor. "We ruined your final."

Motor looked around to make sure nobody was watching. Then he grinned. "Don't worry, I've had this covered all along." He opened up his bag to pull out a quill pen and a few sheets of thick, yellowing paper. "These are blank scrolls. Magically treated paper. Illegal to use in class, but I figure I need all the help I can get."

He jotted down a rune, and the scroll disappeared, turning into a small puff of blue fire. It spread over the pentacle for just a moment before snuffing out, leaving behind a sparkling-clean surface.

Motor made ta-da hands. "Behold. Sridhar's Scouring Flame!"

I high-fived Motor. "It's a regular cheat sheet."

Meticulous dropped the brush in a huff. "Why didn't you use that before I started brushing?!"

"You were enjoying yourself so much?" said Motor.

"How'd you figure out this scroll thing, anyway?" I said.

Motor opened his bag wide enough to show a Little Free Library's worth of books inside. "This school may have fallen on hard times, but the library here is still top-notch. I found a book about runes there. It's simple stuff once you get the hang of it, like coding. Just write some runes in the correct order, and voilà, the magic happens."

I gave him a fist bump. "We should start calling you Magic Me."

Motor grinned. "If I can do it, so can you." He plopped his pen and a blank sheet into my lap. "Part of the test is cleaning the equipment. Why don't you try the flame rune on the brushes? Just enough to dry them."

I took the pen and paper but didn't even know where to start. Drawing was never really my thing. Still, it was nice to hold a piece of paper in my hands again. Out of habit, I folded the sheet instead of drawing on it, making the first shape that came to mind: the fire rune Motor had just drawn.

Motor fidgeted with the tassels of his carpet. "What are you doing?!"

"Oh, this?" I waved the folded origami in the air. "Just goofin'. It's harmless. Watch."

I tossed the paper at Motor's cleaning supplies. "Fire in the hole!"

"This is not a good deed," said the MeMinder X.

As the paper struck Motor's stuff, it bloomed into a fireball, leaping from our spot straight to the teacher table. The scrolls that Lunt and the others had been poring over burst into flames.

That's the thing about jokes on a magical Earth: they tend to have punch lines you never saw coming.

22

Macadamia Me

You'd think extinguishing a small fire would be no sweat for wizard teachers at a magic school. But for that to be true, you'd need a better magic school than the Polymagic Vocational Institute.

Lunt, Pooplaski, and O'Fartly each cast spells that might have put out the flames, if they hadn't cast them all at the same time. Pooplaski conjured a big wad of fire extinguisher foam, but it melted under the miniature rainstorm conjured by Lunt. The storm might have done the trick if O'Fartly hadn't cast a magical gust of air that blew the cloud away and fed the fire. The inferno raged on hotter than ever, gobbling up half the table as the teachers squeaked like baby orcs.

Meticulous couldn't stop laughing. "Look at their faces! Worth the price of admission!"

"You've got to stop it!" Motor hissed at me.

"I don't know how!" I said.

Suddenly, a Twig in a wizard robe much snazzier than ours stepped into the auditorium. She looked confident and beautiful, like all Twigs I'd met, but with the added mystery of magic. She waved her hand, and a wildebeest appeared out of thin air to stand at her side. The creature seemed to be made entirely out of thick wool, and when it leapt onto the burning desk, it unfurled into a huge blanket that snuffed out the flames in a heartbeat.

"Was that like her Patronus?" I asked. "She collects wildebeest dolls and figures, you know."

"Yes, yes, I knew that about her too," said Meticulous. "Stop showing off."

Lunt looked both relieved and embarrassed to see Twig. "If it isn't my top former student, who transferred to Practical Magical Academy. But I'm not bitter about that. What brings you to these parts?"

Before she could answer, Nash strolled in. He wore a snazzy wizard robe too, plus a very smug look on his face. "We'll get to that in a moment," said Nash. "First, are you sure there aren't any more fires you need us to put out for you?"

O'Fartly forced a laugh, but he wasn't fooling anybody.

"This particular fire was just a fluke. And we were on the verge of finding out who started it."

I might have come clean, just to spare the other students the grief. But all those times getting in trouble with the Lunt of my world had hardwired me against fessing up to anything around him.

Motor started shaking from nerves. The guilt was getting to him. Should I have felt guilty too? Was I so far gone to the dark side that I had no remorse?

"Play it cool," said Meticulous, stealing the words from my mouth.

"Actually, I'm rather impressed anybody here could do *real* magic, even by accident," said Nash.

Twig shot him an 85 percent eyebrow arch. "That's very rude. I animated my first golem here."

Nash shrugged. "That was back in this school's glory days."

Sighing, Twig turned to the teachers. "You can still do your investigation. I just need to borrow Macadamia Macon."

"Why do you need Flying Carpet Boy?" asked Lunt. "We have to question him."

Motor squirmed on his flying carpet so much that a bag of Gargoyle Gulps flipped from the cup holder.

"With all due respect, can it wait?" said Twig. "The game is about to start, and Macadamia's on the team."

"We still have a team?" said Lunt. "I thought we were down too many players and had to forfeit."

"I've volunteered to fill in," said Twig. "Where is Macadamia, anyway?"

She looked around until she found Motor. Her eyes went wide when she took in Meticulous and me beside him. But she rolled with it. "Let's suit up," she said. "You can bring your friends. Your doubles can play too. The rules allow it. Right, Nash?"

Nash sighed. "Sure. As long as they've been summoned by the player and not magically modified in any way. But I'm more concerned about you playing on the other team, Twig. You're supposed to be on *my* team."

Twig shook her head. "This school might lose funding if they don't win at least one game this season, and this is their last chance. As a former student here, I'm allowed to step in and play on the team."

"I want you to understand something, Twig," said Nash. "I play to win. I won't be pulling any punches. Even against my favorite point guard."

"Whatever," said Twig.

Nash looked embarrassed, but only for a second. I knew I'd cherish that second for days and weeks to come.

"Are you sure you want to play on a team with Macadamia?" asked Lunt. "Have you considered his . . . background?"

"Good point," said Nash. "We all know how that cousin of his turned out."

Twig ignored him and faced the teachers. "It's simple,"

she said. "If you want to save your school, you have to let Macadamia and the others play on the team with me."

The teachers looked at each other, desperate to drum up a final argument, but they'd run out of ideas. They never stood a chance anyway. Nobody ever won an argument against Twig.

23

Super-Size Me

Meticulous claimed to have a lot of reasons for wanting to ditch the game, but the uniform probably had the most to do with it.

"I'm not wearing that hideous thing!" he said on the locker room bench, scooting away from the denim overalls and worker boots we all had to wear. "This entire game is a bloody waste of time! We need to focus on finding None of Me, not playing some rubbish sport we don't understand! What the devil is *change-a-ball*, anyway?!"

Motor still hadn't explained change-a-ball to us. He'd been too busy rifling through his bag, which was magically bigger on the inside and took forever to search.

"The game won't take long," I said, pulling off my robes. "And we don't want to let the school down."

"Don't insult my intelligence," said Meticulous. "You just want to impress the Twig of this Earth because you struck out with the one on your Earth!"

Something in my head snapped, and I rushed at Meticulous. Even without the fizz, I could take him. He must have had the same idea, because he raised his fists, ready for me.

Before we got any closer, Motor stepped between us, waving a piece of parchment in the air. "Guys, please! This is the clue I told you about, remember? From None of Me's book?"

Meticulous snatched the paper from him and read over it. His eyes widened in surprise. "Why are the runes . . . moving?"

I peered over his shoulder. Sure enough, the runes shifted from one shape to another the longer you looked at them.

"The shapes change in a consistent pattern," said Motor, folding his flying carpet and stuffing it into the pocket of his overalls. "I just can't figure it out."

Meticulous chuckled in that superior way of his. "You've been away from good old dependable science for too long. You simply need an algorithm to calculate the shifts between shapes. Then you can translate it."

"Right!" said Motor. "So can you do that, then?"

"Hmmm, let me think," said Meticulous, cranking up the sarcasm. "We need a calculating machine of some kind. Do they have those on a magic Earth like this one? No? Well, I guess magic can't do everything, can it?"

Embarrassed, Motor dug through his bag and pulled out his MePad. "Haven't used this in months." He blew a cloud of dust off the screen. "Hope the battery hasn't run down." He started snapping shots of the parchment every few seconds.

Meticulous watched the MePad with hungry eyes, like he'd been starving for electronics. "Enough shots and the MePad can sort it out," he said. "I expect it may take a few minutes, though."

"It's like magic and science mixing into something new," I said.

Motor looked thoughtful. "Yeah, that's pretty cool, actually."

Meticulous made a gagging sound. "Let's not get carried away. This is just the MePad doing photo analysis. Magic and science don't mix. Period."

Motor set up the program he needed and launched it. Then he pulled out a bag of Cool Ranch Dragon Scalez and passed them around. I'd learned to trust his judgment in alternate-Earth junk food and didn't hesitate to grab a handful.

Meticulous waved away the snack as he leaned over Motor's shoulder to check the MePad's progress bar. "Half a bloody hour? What kind of grotty processor have you got in this thing?!"

"Guess we've got no choice but to play some change-a-ball," I said, reaching for another handful of Dragon Scalez. "So what exactly is change-a-ball, anyway?"

We'd just finished strapping into our overalls when Twig knocked on the locker room door and stepped inside. She looked far cooler in her uniform than we did in ours.

"Ready?" she said.

We nodded together, which made her laugh. Her smile turned my joints into pudding.

"Sorry, but it's funny when you three are in sync," she said. "Oh, that reminds me. Since we're going to be teammates, we need to be honest with each other. I know you're not really duplicates created by a spell. I know you're from different Earths."

We must have given her the exact same look of total bafflement, because she laughed all over again.

"How did you figure that out?" I asked her.

"I didn't," she said. "I'm best friends with the Meade of this Earth. Before he locked himself away in his tower, he told me all about the different versions of himself and his theories about the Rip and how he wanted to fix it."

"Do tell!" said Meticulous. "What were his ideas?"

Twig munched on a clump of her hair just like I'd seen her do a hundred times. "He didn't go into much detail, just said he'd come up with some magic that might act as a bandage for the Rip until he could find a more permanent solution. After that, he locked himself away in his tower, the vines grew over it, and no one's heard from him since.

That's when all this Dark Lord silliness started up. Just because Meade's not around to defend himself, everyone suspects the worst."

The plucking of a harp wafted through the air.

"That's the pregame lineup alert," said Twig. "We've got to get on the court. On the way, you can tell me why you're here."

As we wound through the halls, we managed to fill Twig in on the highlights of our trip. She laughed at the way Motor and I finished each other's sentences and bickered with Meticulous.

"You three remind me of my Meade, in your own ways," she said.

"So what's your Meade like?" I asked as we approached the player entrance to the stadium. *And just how bad is he?* I wanted to add but didn't.

She smiled to herself. I wondered if my Twig ever smiled like that when she thought about me.

"Meade has a big heart and a good sense of humor," she said, walking up to the door. "And he's never let all his accomplishments go to his head." She opened the door for us. "You know, Me Corp. isn't even his proudest achievement. What really excites him the most is this new type of magic he invented. Origamagic, he calls it."

I would have asked her more about that, but my brain was too busy doing a cliff dive after seeing who stood waiting for us on the other side of the door.

Mom and Dad.

The Mom and Dad of my Earth had done so much *Lord of the Rings* cosplay at comic book conventions that I barely batted an eye at the medieval lord and lady outfits on their counterparts from this Earth. No, what got me was the way they held hands. I hadn't seen them be affectionate like this in ages.

"So it's true," said Mom, taking in us Mes with tears in her eyes. "Meade said there might be echoes of himself from different planes of existence."

Motor and Meticulous had lost their ability to speak. Motor marveled at the sight of Dad, and Meticulous couldn't take his eyes off Mom.

That left the conversation up to me. I didn't know where to start. "Uh, when was the last time you talked to him?"

"A few months ago, soon after people started spreading those baseless accusations that he'd created the Rip," said Dad. "He locked himself away in his tower after that, and we haven't heard from him since. We're worried sick about him. But he said you'd be coming to help. And he wanted us to give you a message."

"The message is this," said Mom. " 'I'll be waiting.' "

Motor butted in. "Do you think he meant 'I'll be waiting' as in, 'Let's hang out,' or 'I'll be waiting' as in, 'I'm going to hurt you when you show up'?"

"Never mind him," I said. "You wouldn't know a password or some other way to get into the tower, would you?"

Mom and Dad shook their heads.

More harp chords wafted overhead.

"Meades!" said Twig. "The game's about to start! Let's get over there!"

"We won't keep you any longer," said Mom, sniffling. "It was nice to see you."

Dad wrapped an arm around Mom for support. "We haven't seen or heard from our son for months," he said, choking up. "Please, do what you can to get him out of that tower and away from whatever experiments have cut him off from the world. Please bring him back to us."

We three Mes nodded. For a Mom and Dad still alive and still together, no promise was too big.

24

Change-a-Ball

Hardly any Polymagic Vocational students and faculty bothered to show up to the change-a-ball game, and those who did had an odd way of showing their school pride. As we ran out onto the court, they made fart noises with their hands.

Meticulous got huffy. "Are they having a go at us?"

"Not at all," Motor told us. "Hand-farts are the way people clap here."

On the sidelines, a goblin girl and boy in cheerleader uniforms droned a chant that seemed to be more about us surviving the game in one piece than about us winning it.

Meanwhile, the visitor side had filled to the max with

Practical Magical Academy fans. Their hand-farts were deafening as Nash and his three equally large and menacing teammates jogged onto the court. Ms. Assan, the drama teacher from my Earth, entered behind them in a cloak with COACH in bright red flames on the back.

"Why don't we have a coach?" I asked Motor.

"Budget cuts," he said, setting his backpack down on the bench.

Twig ran out to shake hands with Nash and consult with the referee, a living tree person in a black-and-white-striped jersey. Motor, Meticulous, and I all snuck a peek at Mom and Dad in their seats up front.

"I still can't get over seeing those two," said Motor. "Especially Dad."

"Quite," said Meticulous, his voice almost tender. "I have my issues with Father, but seeing him comforting Mum like that, well . . ."

"Maybe you could hang out with him or something when you get home," said Motor.

Meticulous shrugged. "Maybe."

I thought about my version of Mom and Dad and what Earth they might be on right now. Were Twig, Lil Battleship, and the rest okay too? I couldn't let myself think about them, or the dung beetles would swarm my insides. So I changed the subject. "What Mom and Dad and Twig said about None of Me made him sound like not such a bad guy after all. You think that's for real? Is he really out to fix the Rip?"

Meticulous bent over to stretch his legs. "If he is, he hasn't succeeded yet."

Motor did a few halfhearted jumping jacks. "They say he's been cursing Me Corp. products."

"Yes, we heard that too," said Meticulous, standing up again. "And I don't believe it. Cursing your own product line makes no business sense. Look, None of Me could be the Dark Lord, he could be the Fuzzy-Wuzzy Lord—it doesn't bloody matter. We just have to find him and get to Earth One."

Twig jogged back over to us. "Hey, triple threat, let's get our heads in the game! It's about to start!"

Mr. Clark, the school janitor on my Earth, stepped onto the court, big white feathery wings sticking out of his back. He carried a ball that changed its shape in his hands, growing as big as a basketball, then as small as a golf ball, then stretching into a football.

Meticulous and I gave Motor the same baffled look.

Motor shrugged. "That's why they call it change-a-ball. It'll make sense in a second. Or not."

Twig looked worried. "You guys went over how to play the game, right?"

"Uh, sure," I said, not wanting to let her down. "It's just, where we come from, the sports equipment tends to stay in one shape."

Twig chewed on a piece of her hair. "No offense, but that sounds pretty boring."

Mr. Clark stretched out his wings to get everybody's

attention. "As principal of this school, I want a good clean game," he told us. "And would the visiting team please go easy on these kids?"

A cocky grin spread across Nash's face.

The tree referee pulled a small harp from his pocket and ran his fingers along the strings.

"Time to play ball!" yelled Mr. Clark, throwing the ball in the air. Nash and Twig both jumped for it, but Nash came away with the prize.

"Medusa ball!" he shouted.

It was like the tablecloth of the world had been pulled out from under us. Basketball hoops rose up on either end of the court as Nash and his teammates sprinted across the floor. The ball they now dribbled and passed to each other had sprouted squirming snake tails all over. I could have sworn I saw a giant set of snake eyes somewhere under all that wriggling. "Don't look it in the eyes!" yelled Twig. "You'll get turned to stone!"

Before Meticulous and I even knew what was happening, Nash shot the creepy ball and scored. I'd felt jealous and resentful every time I'd seen Nash sink a basket back home, but now that I was on the opposing team, I could do something about it. I swore to myself that if I couldn't beat him, I'd at least keep him from trouncing us completely.

"Come on!" yelled Twig on her way down the court. "I need help guarding Nash!"

Motor followed behind her, giving me an apologetic look that said, *Well, that's change-a-ball for you.*

When Twig reached Nash, he kept the ball out of her reach just long enough to shout, "Mace ball!"

The floor sprouted grass, and the basketball hoops widened into soccer goals. The ball morphed to iron as Nash kicked it toward a teammate. Unlike the rest of us, Twig was ready. She stole the ball with her feet and sent it sailing toward Motor.

With the flying carpet in his overall pocket lightening every step he took, Motor reached the ball and lined up a perfect shot. Then we all found out why mace ball was called mace ball: spikes shot from the surface just as his foot connected with it.

Yelping in pain, Motor grabbed his foot and hopped in place. Nash tackled him for no good reason.

The tree referee plucked his harp. "Penalty! Unnecessary roughness!"

Twig called a time-out, and the three of us joined her in a huddle. Before she could dress us down, I cut her off with a question. "I understand now that whoever touches the ball gets to change the game. But if the game is always changing, so is the scoring system, right? How does anybody win?"

Twig gave me a 75 percent eyebrow arch. "Didn't Motor explain this? Or do you Mes just never listen? You have to get the highest score by the time the clock runs out."

"Theoretically, there's another way," said Meticulous,

acting bored. "You could switch to a game like disgraceball and tag all the opposing players out."

"Disgraceball?" I asked.

"I believe it's called dodgeball on your Earth," said Meticulous. "Sports from other Earths count, right?"

Twig looked intrigued. "Maybe. My Meade had the change-a-ball take on all kinds of funky shapes last time we played a one-on-one practice game together. But you can't really tag more than one person in change-a-ball. After you hit somebody, any nearby teammate of theirs could scoop up the ball and shift the game to a different sport."

"Oh, right," said Motor. "It's hopeless, then. We don't stand a chance out there."

Twig punched him on the arm, then Meticulous, then Me. It gave me a warm and fuzzy feeling. And a bruise.

"Buck up!" she said. "The game's not over yet. Let's get back out there and start winning!"

Murmuring agreement, we broke up the huddle and hoofed it back to our positions. On the way there, Meticulous ran alongside me.

"You know the real reason she's doing this, don't you?" he asked.

"She told us already: to help save the school," I said.

"Rubbish!" he said. "She wants to be near us because she fancies None of Me. And with him gone, we're the next-best thing. We remind her of him."

"As if!" Deep down, though, I liked the idea that this Twig

154

might have a thing for None of Me. Then again, if None of Me really was bad, what did that say about her judgment?

"She certainly doesn't fancy Nash, I can tell you that," Meticulous added. "I've never met a Twig who preferred a Nash to one of us."

I couldn't believe Meticulous had actually said something that made me feel better.

The refer-tree strummed the harp again, and the field changed into something like a tennis court, but with lava pits and fire spouts. We had to dodge all sorts of eruptions as we chased the ball. I wound up crashing into the net head-first while Meticulous and Motor bonked into each other.

Everybody in the crowd laughed. I couldn't blame them.

"Look alive, cleaning clones!" said Twig. She reached the ball and shouted "Soot ball!"

The court changed into a football field and the ball became a pigskin that Twig hurled at me. When I caught it, the ball shot a thick cloud of ash in my face. I cleared my eyes just in time for a perfect view of Nash and his teammates barreling down on me. In seconds, they'd steamroll me flat.

My brain did a more elaborate cliff dive than it had before, this one starting with a handstand and followed by a double twist and a triple somersault. I'd never survive this. For about the hundredth time that day, I wished for the fizz to come back.

"Change it up, Average!" yelled Motor.

Change it to what? My mind felt empty as a cardboard box in the rain. The best I could manage was to hurl the ball at Nash, if only for the distraction. Just before the ball left my fingers, an idea occurred to me.

"Dung ball!" I shouted.

The ball changed into a big round hunk of poop as it sailed through the air and smacked Nash's perfect face. It hit him so hard that the dung splattered the rest of his team too.

The ref twanged his harp. "Game over!" he cried.

Nash clawed at the gunk on his face, just like I'd done a few hours before. "Dung ball?! This doesn't count! How can he win just by flinging poop?!"

"By striking every member of your team with a dung ball," said the ref. "That's how the game's been played for centuries by the native dryad population of a world on a different plane from this one."

Mr. Clark puffed up his wing feathers as he addressed the crowd. "Polymagic Vocational wins! This means we get the grant money! We get to stay open!"

Gasps of surprise turned into roars of joy as the crowd poured from the stands and rushed the playing field, hand-farting all the way. Twig ran up to me and almost gave me a hug, then thought better of it. She slugged me in the arm instead.

Motor wasn't so reserved. He pulled me into a bear hug and gave me a noogie. Meticulous nodded in my direction, which, coming from him, might as well have been a standing ovation.

As Motor and Twig recited the blow-by-blow replay of my dung ball maneuver, I looked over to the local version of Mom and Dad. They smiled back at me in a sad sort of way. We waved goodbye to each other as they got up to leave.

The cheering fans hoisted me onto Twig's shoulders. I'd always dreamed of taking in a sea of adoring fans from this sort of view. Oddly enough, those particular daydreams never included the sight of Lunt, O'Fartly, and Pooplaski pushing through the throng with old-timey manacles in hand. Manacles that looked just the right size for a Me.

25

Playing Hooky

Nash, still smeared in poo, shoved people out of the way to clear a path for the teachers dead-set on arresting Motor, Meticulous, and me.

"Stop this celebration!" Lunt yelled.

Everybody went quiet.

"Macadamia Macon and his duplicates are hereby required to report to the dungeon for punishment!" Lunt continued.

As O'Fartly and Pooplaski read out the charges against us from a scroll, Motor broke out a Gnome Gnibbler candy bar. He flipped the unopened snack over and over in his palm. "This is bad," he said. "We'll never get out of this one."

Over at the bench, Meticulous scanned the MePad. The device must have finished its calculations, because he seemed excited by what he read. He gave us a thumbs-up, then pointed to the exit and slipped away.

"He's ditching us?" said Motor.

"No, he just wants us to meet him outside." I hoped I sounded convincing, because I wasn't so sure myself.

Motor gestured to the huge hand-farting crowd surrounding us. "But we can't get out, and you know he'll never wait for us."

"Hang on," said Twig.

She slammed her hands together and bubbles spilled between her fingers. The moment Lunt, Pooplaski, O'Fartly, and Nash broke through the crowd to reach us, Twig opened her arms wide. A blizzard of bubbles filled the air, slamming into the wizards and knocking them off their feet.

The crowd squeezed out a deafening roar of hand-farts.

"This is not a good deed," said the MeMinder X.

"Don't ruin the moment," I told the watch.

Unfurling his flying carpet, Motor eyed my stupid watch. "It has some sort of . . . conscience?"

"Dad added it," I said. "It's mostly just a pain in the butt."

"I don't know, could have its uses." Motor folded his legs crisscross at the front of the carpet as it rose into the air.

Twig turned to me with a familiar grin on her face.

"We owe you one," I told her as I climbed onto the carpet behind Motor. I spilled a few packs of Harpy Honey Hair from yet another cup holder on the way up.

"Do me a favor," Twig said as we rose higher and higher. "Give my Meade a message when you see him. Tell him, 'See ya on the other side.'"

We flew all over the campus looking for Meticulous, but had to leave when they sicced a ghost biker gang on us. By that point, we had no other option but to flee in the direction of Me Corp. Tower.

"He's gonna beat us to None of Me!" I said, dodging a flock of tiny knights jousting with each other on the backs of flapping pigeons.

"Maybe he won't be able to figure out the clue without us," said Motor, weaving the carpet around a group of condos shaped like giant genie bottles.

"He's Meticulous," I said. "He probably figured out the riddle the moment he saw it."

"Well, maybe we'll find him before he makes it there."

We spotted Meticulous a few blocks later getting harassed by a pack of teenage elves outside the Transformed Troll Hair and Beauty Salon. Motor drove the kids off by spraying them with a can of Basilisk Venom Energy Drink as he buzzed overhead.

"Well, if it isn't the deserter," I said as we hovered just out of his reach.

Meticulous waved Motor's MePad in the air. "Don't give me that! I just figured I should clear out before they searched our stuff and found the clue. Plus, I just *had* to change out of that horrible uniform. Couldn't wait. So let me on board already."

Motor and I had fun hemming and hawing about giving him a ride, until Meticulous reminded us that he had the clue we needed to enter the tower. Motor lowered the carpet just enough to let Meticulous hop on.

The carpet sagged lower to the ground with a third passenger, but it flew well enough.

"Why were you letting those elves push you around?" I asked as we buzzed over an off-leash park for pet gremlins.

"Don't you remember?" said Meticulous. "All my skills were just a joke. Turns out I was fizzing all along. And now that I can't fizz, I'm useless. I can't fight back."

"I can't fizz right now either, not in any serious way," I said. "But you don't see me giving up."

Meticulous scoffed. "I'm not *giving up*! I'm just expecting better service from you two next time. Until I can acquire some real bodyguards, you'll have to do."

I probably should have pushed him off the carpet, but he had a point. With my fizz drained away and maybe never coming back, I wasn't good for anything. What did I even contribute to the group? Meticulous had the brains and Motor had the magic. They might decide to just ditch me as dead weight at any moment.

"Why don't you tell us about the MePad's translation of the clue?" Motor asked as we approached Me Corp. Tower.

"About time you asked," said Meticulous. "It's a poem."
He cleared his throat and recited the lines from memory,
like the show-off that he was:

"To escape the green arms
When they give ye pursuit,
Seek ye the magic
That won't let them take root."

"What does that mean?" I asked.

"You tell me," said Meticulous.

"What, you don't plan to contribute?" I asked.

"I've already contributed a great deal and will continue
to do so," said Meticulous. "But riddles bore me and I don't
do rhymes."

We circled around Me Corp. Tower and saw the moving
vines up close. They wriggled up and down the building, as
thick around as people and covered in thorns the size of traffic cones. News crews swarmed the front entrance, so Motor
landed the carpet in the back parking lot. We couldn't get
too close for fear the vines would grab us.

The sight of all those squirmy, thorny tentacles brought
out the pessimist in Motor. "This is hopeless," he said. "We'll
never get past that plant monster."

"But we've got the clue," said Meticulous. "Surely you
two gits can figure it out."

" 'Seek ye the magic that won't let them take root,' " said
Motor. "It sounds like a medieval gardening manual."

162

"That's it!" I said. "Vinegar!"

"What's magic about vinegar?" said Meticulous.

"You both helped Aunt Anna in her garden that one spring, right?" I said.

"All I remember is the sunburn," said Motor.

Meticulous shuddered. "And the grit that got under my fingernails."

I rolled my eyes at both of them. "Remember how she killed weeds? She used vinegar and wouldn't shut up about it. She said it was true gardening *magic.* This might be None of Me's idea of an inside joke for us Mes."

"Not a very funny joke," said Meticulous. "And even if you're right, where do we get vinegar?"

Motor pulled a spray bottle full of blue liquid from his bag. The label read WINDOW CLEANER.

"Good for you," said Meticulous. "Now we just have to find some windows to clean."

Motor shook the bottle and the liquid turned clear. The label now read VINEGAR. "It's an Every-Spray bottle," he said. "Standard issue for all students at Polymagic Vocational."

"But that's a small bottle," said Meticulous. "And those are big vines."

Motor twisted the stream knob at the tip of the nozzle as he walked up to the first vine in our path. He pumped the handle and, against all reason, a stream as thick and strong as a fire hose shot from the bottle.

The vine shrank back like a time-lapse video of kudzu

growth in reverse. As Motor kept spraying, enough of the green went away to reveal the rear door.

I'd been expecting a thick wooden door like the kind that led to a dungeon or a dangerous tavern. What I got was the standard, boring glass door of a modern office building, complete with bland stainless-steel trim.

The door didn't even creak when we opened it. All was silent save for the MeMinder X: "This is not a good deed."

"Yeah," I told the watch. "What else is new?"

26

The Chosen One

We walked into Me Corp. to find Hollywood sprawled on a sofa in the lobby, eating from a bowl of Minotaur Munch mini bars perched on his stomach. Flakes of chocolate and caramel had wedged into the links of the chain mail armor he wore.

Hollywood looked even more dumbstruck than usual. "Gee whillikers, guys, if you'll pardon my French!"

He leapt to his feet and started in for a hug. Then he noticed Meticulous. He tugged on the sword at his side, but it wouldn't come out. After a few more tries, the entire sword belt popped open and the whole shebang clattered to the floor. "Fiddlesticks!" He hurled the candy bar at Meticulous instead.

Meticulous caught the treat with one hand. It would have missed him anyway.

Hollywood stamped his booted foot. "What's *he* doing here?"

"Trust me, we can hardly believe it's him either," I said. "But we're more or less stuck with each other."

Meticulous read the nutrition information on the bar wrapper, not bothering to look up. "Hello, assistant."

"Gosh darnit, hello yourself!" said Hollywood. "And I'm not your assistant anymore!"

"Right, right, you're a reality star now," said Meticulous. "So tell me, Chosen One, where's None of Me? Have you challenged the so-called Dark Lord to the big climactic match your viewers want to see?"

Hollywood grabbed another Minotaur Munch bar from the bowl. "As a matter of fact, I've been waiting here to build some suspense for my viewers. I don't want to rush the big finale."

"In other words, the elevator's locked and you can't find the stairs to take you to the top floors so you can face your adversary," said Meticulous. "So much for the big finale."

Hollywood fell back into the sofa and draped his forearm over his eyes as if acting out a Shakespearean death scene. "Fudge! This is bad. This is really bad. My reputation is ruined! I'll never work in this town, or on this Earth, again!"

If I didn't snap Hollywood out of this, he'd be wallowing in melodrama all day. "Well, you were clever to make it this far," I said. "How *did* you get into the building, anyway?"

Hollywood peeked at me from under his arm. "Oh, that. When I first came out here a few days ago, I circled all around the building, trying to figure out a way in. Then I had to relieve myself, if you know what I mean."

"Take a wee?" asked Meticulous.

Hollywood cringed. "Please don't use that language. Anyway, that's when I found out the vines don't like *urine.*" He said it like a bad word, which, on his Earth, it might very well have been.

"You peed your way to the entrance?!" I asked. "That's awesome!"

His face went red. "I'd had a lot of Fairy Fountain Soda that day. Fairy Fountain is one of the show's sponsors. Or they were. They'll be sure to pull their advertising now. My career is ruined!"

"Why should you care?" said Meticulous. "It's not your Earth."

Hollywood tossed his Minotaur Munch wrapper at a wastebasket. He missed. "I'm always pigeonholed as the comic relief. For once I wanted a dramatic role I could really sink my teeth into."

Meticulous pointed to a nearly full wastebasket of wrappers. "And in the end, all you've sunk your teeth into are these bars."

That didn't help Hollywood's mood, so I steered the

conversation toward our mission to fix the Rip, with a rundown of everything that had happened to us so far. It took his mind off his problems, and soon enough, Hollywood was back to himself with such probing, insightful questions as, "What were the Mes at Me HQ wearing?" and "What products does Prez use in his hair?"

Meticulous, exasperated, marched over to the elevator. "Enough of this! We need to find a way upstairs!" He popped open the elevator control panel but looked confused by what he found inside. "What?! No wires? Motor, can you make sense of this? There's a bunch of . . . little people running around down there."

"It's an imp engine!" Excited, Motor pulled from his bag a small metal tin labeled SATYR SPRINKLES and dumped a stream of rainbow candy into the panel. "You can usually bribe them back to work with sugar."

"And then what?" asked Hollywood. "We take on None of Me by ourselves? You guys can't fizz, and Motor and I have always been useless in a fight."

"Well, remember, Twig and his parents don't think None of Me is bad," I said.

"Yeah, but they're Twig and his parents," said Hollywood. "Of course they're gonna say nice things. Too bad we don't have Resist with us. She could take him on."

"When was the last you heard from her?" I asked.

"Like never?"

"We'll look for her after this," I said. "No Me gets left behind."

Hollywood gave me a weird look. "I'm glad you're back, Average, but there's something different about you."

"Uh, something good, I hope?"

But I never found out the answer, because the elevator dinged and the door slid open. Motor and Meticulous took a bow.

"Going up?" they said together. Great, now those two were jinxing too.

27

Mr. Fartz

Compared to getting blown up, zapped to the wrong Earth, nearly drowned, and all the other bad things that had happened to us in an elevator, listening to Hollywood gripe as we rose to the top floor wasn't as bad as it could have been.

"Stupid show," Hollywood muttered. "Should never have signed that stupid contract! After this, I'll be a laughing-stock forever."

Meticulous snorted. "Are you implying your biggest ambition was to be a reality-TV star?"

"Hey, it beats 'stealing inventions from other Earths for fun and profit' as a life goal," I said.

I traded high fives with Motor and Hollywood as Meticulous rolled his eyes.

"It's not like doing a reality show was the be-all and end-all for me," said Hollywood. "But it was supposed to be a step toward bigger things."

"Then take the next step anyway and stop whingeing about it!" said Meticulous. "What good does it do to worry about what anybody else thinks? Motor made a complete plank of himself at that magic school of his, but he kept plugging along without a gripe. And now he has the distinction of being the most wanted arsonist to ever drop out of that place."

Motor blinked. "Um, thanks?"

"And look at Average," said Meticulous. "Leaving all you Mes behind and being locked up for a crime he didn't commit has done a number on him. He's saddled with guilt and uncertainty about his moral compass. But he carries on, trying to do the right thing, no matter how miserable his existence may be."

His words were a dropkick to my gut, but I had no time to stew over them—the elevator slowed to a stop, and the door rumbled open. "After you," said Meticulous, finger on the Open button.

The room we tiptoed into looked like a lab designed by a mad scientist on a shopping spree at Ikea. Chemical concoctions bubbled and burned in tastefully designed glassware. Old and musty spell books lined the simple yet elegant shelves. The tasteful end tables and cabinetry, all of it matching, held a mess of magical odds and ends: glowing gems of power, rows of staffs and wands, a couple of giant hovering eyeballs. But I couldn't take my eyes off a black cloak draped around a mannequin in the corner. It seemed to be made out of hundreds of tiny origami meshed together. A cable ran from the hem of the cloak, along the floor, and outside a window, where it attached to an antenna mounted on the wall. As I watched, a bolt from the Rip struck the antenna, sending a surge of power to the cloak. The origami seemed to ripple and flow. If this wasn't origamagic, I didn't know what was.

"Why is None of Me, um, charging his clothes with the Rip?" I asked.

Meticulous ignored the question as he shoved me aside. He made a beeline for the big metal box in the center of the room that hung in the air, flying-carpet-style. It looked like a cross between a floating coffin and a covered litter box. Electric wires and blinking lights ran along its sides, which gave the thing a scientific vibe that didn't really click with the glowing green runes carved into the lid. I hadn't been around magic long, but I could feel the power wafting from those mystic symbols.

"Is this a magic thing, or a machine thing?" asked Hollywood, standing beside me.

Motor whistled as he took it all in. "Maybe it's a little bit of both."

"This is the Stitch!" Meticulous orbited the box, eyeing every inch of the thing like it was a package that had arrived damaged. "He stole the Stitch from my lab! And vandalized it!"

Meticulous reached out to touch one of the runes on the lid. It flared green sparks, singeing his hand. He shoved his fingers in his mouth and growled.

"*That's* the Stitch?" I said. "How did it end up here?"

Meticulous slammed his fist on the lid, activating two more runes. They would have burned off his hand if he hadn't yanked it away in time. "None of Me nicked it! That chav really is a dark wizard! Look how he ruined my beautiful creation!"

"How does it feel to have someone steal from you for once?" said Hollywood.

Meticulous probably deserved to hear that, but this was all so creepy that nobody laughed.

"Are you sure None of Me meant to ruin the Stitch?" said Motor. "Maybe he was trying to get it to work. You said yourself that you hadn't finished it."

Meticulous waved his hand at his creation in pure disgust. "Rubbish!"

"Motor's right: he did make the effort of going all the way to your Earth and bringing it here," I said.

"Exactly!" said Motor. "I know enough about runes to recognize that these are superpowerful. He might have been using them to finish the Stitch. Maybe he picked up with magic where you left off with science."

"Enough with this science-meets-magic nonsense!" yelled Meticulous. "It's a grotty idea!"

We all went quiet as a door at the far end of the room creaked open. And a devil stepped through.

He was big, beefy, and shirtless, with skin the color of leftover cranberry sauce and horns straight off the alpha ram on the tallest mountain in the world.

"Could you guys keep it down in here?" said the devil. "The boss has some important work to do."

"It's okay," said a distracted voice from the room behind him. "Send them in."

With a sinister smile, the devil held the door open and waved us inside. Meticulous marched right on through, still so irate about the Stitch that not even a demonic creature from the underworld could bother him now. Hollywood, Motor, and I opted to hang back.

"None of Me must be the Dark Lord after all!" whispered Hollywood. "He's in league with Papa Evil!"

"Is that what they call the devil on your Earth?" I asked, eyeing those thick and pointy horns.

"Where I'm from, he's called the Absolute Worst Host," said Motor.

The devil cleared his throat, and we took the hint. Shaking at the exact same frequency, the three of us shuffled past him.

We stepped into an office that looked a lot like the one Meticulous used back on Earth One. Same modern furniture, same fancy art. The difference was that all of this décor moved. The chairs, sofas, and tables scooted out of each other's way so a crew of full-size broom people could sweep and dust. As they bustled about, the lines and colors of the paintings changed from cave drawings to oil portraits to abstract shapes.

The only thing that didn't change was a desk near the window and the hooded wizard who sat there, glancing at a bunch of crystal balls lined up in front of him. Under all that glass I could make out flowcharts, calendars, product shots, and other businessy stuff.

"Would you look at that?" Hollywood whispered. "His chair's normal! I was expecting it to be made out of swords or skulls or something!"

None of Me looked up from a sphere with a set of blueprints titled SELF-FLYING UMBRELLA. "Thanks for bringing them in, Mr. Fartz."

"Mr. Fartz?" whispered Motor.

"Why's this devil named after every Me's favorite stuffed animal?" Hollywood whispered back.

From the depths of his hood, None of Me smiled at his demonic assistant. "On your way out, don't forget to check in with the MeSphere X development team about installing those new curses we talked about. And let me know how much more money we can divert to boost that contribution to the Talking Tree Forest Relief Fund."

Mr. Fartz bowed. "You got it, boss. Have a good chat." Then he disappeared in a puff of sulfur.

When the smoke cleared, None of Me leaned back in his

chair, regarding us from under his hood. "I've been waiting a long time for this day to come."

Meticulous marched up to the edge of the desk and folded his arms over his chest. "You have, have you?"

None of Me chuckled.

"Hey!" said Hollywood. "What's so funny? I'm the Chosen One!"

None of Me pulled off his hood. That is to say, her hood.

This Me was a she, a particular she who everyone in the room knew well.

Resist Me.

28

Business as Usual

Resist whipped out a slingshot from the pocket of her wizard robe and pointed it at Meticulous. Somehow, she looked even scarier with a puny slingshot than she had with a hood over her face and a devil at her side.

"Back away from them!" She flicked the ball in the sling with her thumb, and it lit up like the head of a match. Now she aimed a flaming missile at Meticulous.

"Resist, what are you doing here?" I asked.

"She was the Dark Lord all along!" said Hollywood. "She was playing us!"

Resist rolled her eyes. "It's good to see you too, Hollywood."

"I see what's going on here," said Meticulous. "Resist made her way into this tower, found the Dark Lord gone, and took over his identity, including his business operations." He picked up one of the crystal balls, which showed a financial chart with an arrow shooting upward. "Who would have thought that the most anticorporate, down-with-authority, money-is-evil Me would have such a head for business?"

Resist glared at him. "Would somebody please explain why he's here?!"

So I told her. Resist took it all in, never taking her aim off Meticulous. When I finished, she tightened her grip on her flaming slingshot. "I haven't fully explored this building, but I'm told it's built on top of an old-fashioned dungeon. There's probably a cell down there that would be just perfect for Meticulous."

"That's a tempting offer," I said. "But you've gotta tell us what happened to you. Is it true that you took over None of Me's operation?"

"This is his place, all right," said Resist, eyes still on Meticulous. "Everything's pretty much how I found it when I broke in here awhile back."

"Including the Stitch?" asked Meticulous. "Don't look at me like you don't know what I'm talking about!"

"It's the giant floating litter box in that room back there," I said.

"Litter box?" asked Hollywood. "Is that your Earth's word for *scoop-a-poop*?"

"On my Earth we call it Pray-the-Cat-Goes-Here-and-Not-in-the-Plant," said Motor.

Resist chuckled. "You may not believe this, but I've missed you guys. Anyway, the Stitch thing was there when I got here. Along with all that other stuff."

"How did you even get in?" said Motor. "We had to solve a riddle and everything."

"So did I!" said Hollywood.

"No you didn't," said Meticulous. "You just took a wee like a little child."

Resist flicked the flaming pellet in her sling again. The flames rose higher. "Hey, Fancy Pants! Nobody gets to make fun of Hollywood but me. Got it?"

Meticulous just scowled at her, trying not to look impressed.

"So, you were about to tell us how you got into the tower," said Motor.

"Oh, that," said Resist. "I just sort of jumped and dodged the vines and thorns as they came at me. You know, my usual thing. Not that it was easy or anything. I'm not sure if the scratches will ever heal all the way. But I got inside and found all his stuff. And I met Mr. Fartz. That's not his real name, in case you were wondering. Apparently, None of Me gave him the nickname, because his name is unpronounceable or cursed or something."

Hollywood made a squeamish face. "So, does None of Me make it a habit of summoning evil things? And does that make him evil?"

Resist shook her head. "That's a negative stereotype about otherworldly beings. Let's keep an open mind. Just think of Mr. Fartz as a genie with an edgy look. He's an invaluable executive assistant."

"Does he know where None of Me went off to?" I asked.

"Not a clue," said Resist. "Before I got here, None of Me ordered all his employees to work from home and sealed off the building with the vine curse. He claimed he had a big emergency to research and couldn't be disturbed. Mr. Fartz tried to disturb him anyway a few days later but found that his boss had disappeared."

Meticulous ran his fingers along the line of crystal balls on the desk. "So where do you fit into this? When did you sell your soul to the devil and take over the business in None of Me's place?"

For a second, Resist looked like she might shoot Meticulous. Instead, she blew out the flaming ball and lowered the weapon. "You're lucky my hand's getting tired. I'm a quick draw, though, so no funny stuff."

Meticulous tried to look unconcerned, but you could see she'd gotten the message through.

"It is a little odd, though, you've got to admit," I told her. "You've spent so much time protesting the powers that be. And now, well, you're the one with the power."

Resist stuffed her slingshot back into her pocket, then picked up four of the crystal balls and started juggling them. Her technique was as smooth as Rodeo Clown Me's. "Tell me about it. When I first stumbled into this place, I planned to just burn it all to the ground. But then Mr. Fartz introduced himself. He was under orders from None of Me to hand control of Me Corp. over to the first Me who walked through the door."

"If you had control of the business and you hated it so much, why didn't you close it down or something?" asked Hollywood.

Meticulous barked a laugh. "You can't just shut down a corporation! There are investors to answer to! A board of directors!"

"And all those normal, working-class people who work for us," said Resist, speeding up her juggling. "I couldn't take away their jobs. Plus, I realized that through all the products Me Corp. provides, we reach *a lot* of people."

"Ha!" said Meticulous. "Here's where she gets tempted by the power and money that's been thrust into her lap."

Resist snatched up a fifth ball and added it to the mix with no problem. "Hardly. I decided to curse the products Me Corp. makes."

Hollywood backed up until he bumped into an ottoman cruising past him. "So you *have* gone evil!"

Motor's eyes went wide. "I didn't think the rumors were true."

"Let's hear her out, people," I said. "Explain, please."

Resist did a loop-de-loop with the spheres, juggling them in the opposite direction. "Thanks, Average. I've had our research team develop curses for our products that only affect very specific users. That is, any person trying to do bad things with our technology. So, for instance, propagandists and meme-makers who spread phony news and other fake information get cursed to tell only the truth. Trolls who insult and attack other people online lose the use of their voice."

"As a celebrity who's gotten raked over the coals by trolls and haters, I love this!" said Hollywood.

Resist threw the balls higher without breaking her flow. "We're even harsher on other companies."

"Now I see what game you're playing!" said Meticulous. "You're cursing the competition!"

"Not at all," said Resist. "We just curse the executive teams and boards of directors at companies doing sleazy things. Like the company bigwigs who make their apps addictive on purpose. They're consigned to lose their ability to focus or concentrate on anything."

"Nice!" said Motor. "But how long do these curses last?"

Resist put some spin on the spheres so they each arced in different patterns as she kept tossing them. "The curses last until the accursed learn their lessons. Hopefully this will help slow down the destructive tendencies of these corporations and capitalism in general—"

"Okay, we get it," said Hollywood. "No need for one of your speeches."

Meticulous raised his hand. "And let the record show that I definitely think capitalism is a good thing!"

"We don't want to hear your spiel, Meticulous," I said.

"So, Resist, why did you go it alone? Motor and Hollywood were here for weeks."

Resist caught the balls one by one and plopped them back on the desk. "The building's magically sealed off from the world, remember? I've been trapped and making the best of it. But trust me, I was worried about you guys too."

"Awwww," said Hollywood, leaning in for a hug.

Resist pulled away him. "I'm not gonna get *that* sappy."

"On to more pressing matters," said Meticulous. "That antenna rigged outside. It's to charge the Stitch, right?"

"That and other things," said Resist. "Like the cloak. Plus some glowing piece of paper I'm too afraid to touch."

Meticulous made a gagging sound. "Portal paper! I had a prototype lying around my office. The wally must have nicked that from my Earth too! With it, I can finally bring the Stitch to Earth Zero!"

"You want to go back there?!" said Hollywood. "Geez Louise! And I don't care who hears me say it!"

"That's been our final destination all along," said Meticulous. "That's where the Rip originated. That's where we have to launch the Stitch. Otherwise, it won't work."

"I'm all for helping the Mes and stopping the Rip, but I'm not trusting Meticulous to do it," said Resist. "Have we forgotten that he's the one who made the Rip in the first place?"

Meticulous turned to me with a hurt look that would have made me feel sorry for him, if he weren't Meticulous. "Average, do you feel this way too?"

On the one hand, I'd come this far with Meticulous and wanted to see our mission through. On the other, I still didn't like him. More to the point, I still didn't trust him.

"We just need more information," I said. "You haven't even explained how the Stitch works. How are we supposed to know if it's really going to fix the Rip?"

"It does look an awful lot like a weapon," said Motor.

With a huff, Meticulous marched to the door. "We've wasted more than enough time here! You can keep having a go at me if you like, but I'm gone!"

And with that, Meticulous left the room and slammed the door behind him.

Resist shook her head. "How have you survived a whole day with him?"

"It hasn't been so bad," I said. "Well, okay, it has."

"Do you really think this Stitch thing is for real?" said Hollywood.

"I've been peddling magic for months now, and even I don't see how you can just blast something into the Rip and, presto, it's all fixed." Resist snapped her fingers.

"Then again, the origami drive seemed pretty unlikely too, until he invented it," said Motor.

"Yeah," I said. "And he's been pretty dedicated to getting this thing done. I can't believe I'm saying it, but I think he's changed. It defies all reason, but he actually made a friend."

Before I could tell them all about Cave, a green light flashed under the door.

"What's that?!" said Motor.

I wasn't sure if I guessed the truth so much as I felt it in my bones. "The portal paper! I didn't think he'd use it without us!"

We raced to the door and flung it open, crashing into each other on our way out.

In the center of the room, the last light of a portal shrank away into nothing. You could still see the traces in the air showing how it had been big enough for a person to fit through. A person and his Stitch. The reality of it all set in: Meticulous had left with the Stitch. And with it, our only chance of ever escaping this Earth.

29

Leave Me Be

When I'd agreed to help Meticulous, I'd truly hoped that
he'd changed. At least, I'd hoped he'd been capable of
change. Maybe on some level I'd even thought we could
come out of this as friends, or hate each other a little less.

But in the end, my evil-genius alternate-Earth double
had stabbed me in the back again.

Motor, Resist, and even Hollywood spared me their
I-told-you-sos. They left me alone to wallow in my thoughts
as they ransacked None of Me's office to find anything that
might help us get off this Earth. Resist swore she'd seen
more portal paper in a drawer, but it turned out to be wrap-
ping for a gift-giving holiday called Goblin Grab.

Motor climbed out of a bigger-on-the-inside filing cabinet he'd squeezed his entire body into. The sounds of monsters roaring and screeching echoed from its metal depths. "Yep, we're stranded," he said. "We may as well just forget it."

"Now, now, we'll have none of that." Resist unfolded some origami fantasy creatures she'd found in a drawer to see if any turned out to be portal paper. No such luck. "You're not turning back into Mr. Surrender. You're the most confident I've ever seen you, and I want you to stay that way. We *will* get out of here."

Rifling through an old desk, Hollywood yanked his fingers away from an enchanted stapler that snapped at him. "Yeah, we could make our own origami drive if we have to. How hard could it be?"

Instead of falling deeper into the dumps along with me, Motor lit up. "That's it! We've had a way to make portals all along!"

"We have?" asked Hollywood.

Motor turned to me. "Average can make them with his mind!"

Resist growled. "I thought Hollywood was the one with the stupid ideas."

"Yeah!" said Hollywood, whacking at the stapler with a glowing letter opener he'd found. "Hey!"

Motor shut the filing cabinet behind him, and the monster noises from inside stopped. "Hear me out. What is the origami drive, anyway? Basically it's just a thing that collects transdimensional energy. Right?"

Hollywood slammed a big spell book over the stapler, pinning it in place. "You lost me at *transdimensional energy.*"

"That's the stuff that can make portals, and it's inside Average," said Motor. "He's like a walking, talking origami drive. No need for an elevator, no need for portal paper. There's every reason to think that Average can do what the origami drive does on his own."

"But how?" I said.

"You've already done it!" said Resist.

Hollywood placed both hands on the spell book and leaned on it to hold the stapler in place. "Confused here!"

"From what you told us about how you left your Earth, Average, it sounds like you didn't even finish folding the portal paper," said Motor.

"Right!" said Resist. "And the portal paper on Earth Zero got *torn* before you even had a chance to finish it!"

Hollywood leapt away from the desk just as the stapler broke free of the book and came at him again. "Oh, I get it now! Whether it was from lightning or torn portal paper, Average got covered in transdimensional goop when he was thinking about origami keys. So he wound up accidentally turning that goop into portals both times."

We all stared at Hollywood, stunned.

"What?" he said, knocking the stapler into a garbage can with one swipe of the book. "I can figure out things too."

"But even if that's what really happened, it's not like I can repeat those accidents," I said. "Plus, I've lost most of my fizz. Unless somebody has a Me recharging station lying around, I won't have enough juice."

Resist nodded at the cloak across the room. "That should do the trick."

Hollywood shrank from the garment. "That's the Dark Lord's cloak! I mean, even if None of Me isn't really the Dark Lord, it's still supposed to be an evil, cursed thing. Like the Shadow Blade. And we all know you have to be really bad to be able to use the Shadow Blade."

This didn't seem like the time to mention my own go-around with that particular enchanted item.

"It's just a superstition," said Resist. "None of Me's cloak is more like a wearable battery. From what I can figure, it charges through that cable every time a bolt from the Rip strikes the antenna outside. His notes even label it as his Fizzing Cloak."

"Seriously?" I asked. "He calls it fizzing too?"

"Guess you guys have something in common!" said Hollywood.

Was that a good thing or a bad thing?

I wasn't keen to try on a cursed evil wizard cloak. What if it electrocuted me or took over my mind or turned me into a chicken? But I had no other choice if I wanted to get us out of there. Shaking all over, I walked up to the cloak and touched it. A surge ran through my palm, so I yanked my hand away. It felt like the goop in the origami drive, and I wasn't a fan of that stuff after being trapped in it.

I started to tell my friends I couldn't wear this dangerous

thing, but when I saw the hope on their faces, I knew I had to try again. They'd spent months here, trapped far from their homes, worried about what their versions of Mom and Dad and Twig must have been thinking. Compared to what they'd been through, I had no room to complain. I had to get over myself and do what I could to help them. As Meticulous might have said if he'd been there: "Quit your whingeing!"

Though it felt like poison in my hands, I picked up the cloak and put it on. As it settled over my head and shoulders, the fizz came roaring back to me like a shot of nitro in a *Fast & Furious* movie.

I felt great, but I must have looked pretty intense. At the sight of me in my new getup, Hollywood tiptoed to his customary hiding place behind Resist. "Are you evil now?" he asked.

"I don't feel evil." My voice came out deep and scary, as if it had been auto-tuned for singing in a Norwegian death metal band.

"This is not a good deed," said the MeMinder X.

"I didn't even do anything yet!" I told the watch.

"He really has gone evil!" said Hollywood. "What sort of monster have we created?!"

"Don't be silly!" said Resist. "He's still Average, right?"

"Uh, right," said Motor, looking a little less than convinced.

"I'm fine," I said in that stupid voice again. "The fizz is back too."

"Good!" said Hollywood. "Uh, so now what?"

"Now you've got to repeat everything you did those other times you made portals but didn't know it," said Resist. "Easy, right?"

I had a sarcastic reply ready to go but never got the chance to use it. The origami key for Earth Zero came to me in a flash: a chimera, the three-headed mythological monster. I'd folded the thing before without even realizing it during the desperate escape from Youth Development on my Earth. Now I had to fold it again—in my mind. With the fizz swirling around my head, I imagined the body, the legs, and all three heads into being.

With the final fold, I felt a last trickle of the cloak's energy pass into me like the dregs of a smoothie when you tip it back into your mouth. I knew the fizz would fade from me any second, so I used what was left to push the chimera from my head and into the real world.

And somehow it worked. A glowing green chimera floated in front of my eyes before it unfurled into a familiar green hole in reality.

"Okay, guys," I told my friends, my voice back to normal. "Let's go find that *manky prat* Meticulous."

30

Mystery Me

After stepping through a portal from a dark wizard's tower in the heart of a magical kingdom, the last place I expected to end up was my bedroom.

Not that it was *my* bedroom per se. It belonged to either President Me or some different Me whose house had been dumped on Earth Zero. Whoever the Me was, he'd grown up here surrounded by the things I'd owned all my life too. The same secondhand desk where I avoided homework, the same drum set I was too lazy to play, the same T.U.F.F. Puppy bedsheets I could never bring myself to throw out. And more or less the same comic books, just with different names (*Bat Person, The Incredible Bulk, The Not-Really-All-That-Fantastic Four*).

The only change that really stood out was the movie poster for *Star Peace,* featuring all the characters from Star Wars, good and bad, chumming it up like buddies in a comedy. But I was so homesick I didn't mind, and neither did the other Mes. We gathered around the familiar dresser to look at pictures of us as kids and make fun of our old hairstyles. I laughed along with them, though deep down I couldn't stop wondering when the last time was that I'd felt so innocent and happy. When had I taken the path that had led to me turning out so rotten? Was I even a Me anymore, now that I'd gone so close to the dark side? I noticed the way Resist, Hollywood, and even Motor had given me extra space since I'd put on the evil-wizard cloak. It was only a matter of time before they rejected me altogether.

Hollywood pointed out a picture of the Me mugging with Twig at the annual county fair. "That was the day Twig stuck sugar clouds in my ears."

"You mean cotton candy?" I asked.

"Oh, that's what you call it?" said Resist. "On my Earth, it was known as edible fiberglass before it got banned altogether. My Earth's not so fun, FYI."

"You know how it is where I come from," said Motor. "They call it Five Grams of Sugar and You're Still Hungry."

We all laughed. But not for long.

"Ugh, what's that smell?" said Resist.

All our noses curled the same way.

"That's exactly how the gosh-darned house smelled that time I flooded it," said Hollywood.

"You flooded Mom and Dad's house?!" said Resist.

Mumbling something about an accident, Hollywood moved on to a less embarrassing topic. "Are we even sure this is Earth Zero?" He peeled back a curtain to reveal a boarded-up window.

Doubt crept into my head. "Making portals just by thinking is a new thing for me. Maybe I sent us to the wrong place?"

Motor opened a closet full of hazmat suits and gas masks. "Do people on Earth Zero dress like this?"

"Could you imagine having to wear that?" said Hollywood. "A gas mask doesn't go with anything!"

"We'd better see what's out there," said Resist.

Nervous, the four of us stepped into the hall and took the familiar stairs. Down on the first floor, it reeked even more than above. The carpet and furniture had rotted, and gray water stains lined the walls.

Hollywood surveyed the damage like some no-nonsense tool pro in an orange shirt at Home Depot. "Looks like flooding, all right."

On our way to the front door, we passed the ruined kitchen where Mom and Dad had told me about the Janus Hotel the day I first went to Me Con. Now that seemed like a lifetime ago. I reached out to touch the last unbroken *Battlestar Galactica* collectible bowl from Mom and Dad's nerd cupboard. I'd eaten cereal out of a bowl just like this too many mornings to count.

When my fingers touched the Cylon pictured on the side, my head fizzed with the vision of a flooded city, its buildings drowning under a harsh sun. I'd seen this Earth before.

"Earth One Hundred Fourteen!" I said. "That flooded Earth I mentioned that got seriously messed up by climate change! That's where this house is from!" Where was the Me who lived here? Had he moved on? Had he survived?

Hollywood, who'd been about to open the door, yanked his hand off the knob like it might burn him. "We're on a flooded world?!"

"Get a grip!" said Resist, scooting around him to reach the door. "Even if that's where we are, it's dry now."

"The real question is whether Meticulous is out there or he wound up somewhere else," said Motor.

"If he is here, he can't have gotten far," said Resist, turning the doorknob. "We just have to figure out which way he headed after he got out."

We had our answer the moment she opened the door. Across the street, in front of a store called Lamps R Us, Meticulous struggled to break out of a giant glass lightbulb that held him like a cage.

31

Mediocre Me

Overhead, the Rip blazed in the sky, bigger and meaner than ever. Rows of stacked garbage stretched out in every direction. Big Ben's digital alarm screeched in the distance. This was Earth Zero all right, specifically the junkyard of the multiverse.

We seemed to be in a section of the junkyard where whole buildings had come to roost. Lamps R Us across the street was part of a strip mall full of other shops that nobody would ever want to visit: Ketchup Emporium, Custom Coffins While U Wait, Nothing but Tofu, Cautious Sam's Safe and Practical Fireworks.

Motor craned his neck back and forth to take it all in. "This place is just as wild as you said, Average!"

"Quite," Meticulous said from inside his lightbulb prison. "They call it Mediocre Valley, where some of the most boring bits and bobs in the entire multiverse have ended up. Makes the place a good hideout for my captors, since no one thinks to come here."

Hollywood tapped the glass of the bulb. "What seems to be the problem, *boss*? I thought you could escape any prison better than Escape Me. Oh, right, that was only when you had superpowers."

"Get me out of here, *now*!" Meticulous growled.

Motor pointed to the Stitch a few doors down. It had drifted in front of a hotel made entirely out of packing foam. "Guess you're pretty desperate to get back your toy."

Meticulous pounded on the glass. "Yes, yes, now get me out! They're coming back any second!"

"Who?" I asked.

The Lamps R Us door opened and out walked a living cartoon. He had a head at least twice as large as it should have been, way out of proportion with his body. But I'd know that face anywhere, just as I recognized the *Lord of the Rings* getup he wore.

"Ren Faire Me?" said Hollywood, catching on at the same time I did. "You look horrible!"

That wasn't the best thing to say to an

angry bobblehead version of yourself. Ren Faire tilted his huge head from side to side, cracking his neck like a bad guy in a bad movie as he drew his sword.

Resist pulled out her slingshot and aimed it at Ren Faire. Motor did the same with the spray bottle, now full of a fizzy purple liquid.

"Such a lively jest, to be sure!" bellowed Ren Faire. He tended to bellow everything. "Mayhap thou would not be laughing if thou had been cursed too."

Meticulous sighed. "I've told you already—it's not a curse. It must be a mutation caused by too much Rip exposure, probably from when the elevator blew up on you blokes."

Ren Faire shuddered, his massive head wobbling like a loose globe on its pedestal. "Verily, the foul green lightning that zapped us when we crashed did indeed change us all."

"What do you mean, changed you all?" I asked.

The rest of the Viral Mes stepped out of Ketchup Emporium. To look at them, *Monster Mes* might have been a better nickname for this bunch. Troll Me, never the most handsome Me to begin with, had developed the face of an actual troll, from his sloping forehead to his jutting jaw and all the green skin in between. Mobster Me, in his pin-striped suit, now sported a rat head, nose twitching and fangs scraping against each other. Creepiest of all, Click Me and Dare Me now had TV screens attached to their necks, showing their pasty faces in full HD.

"You all look horrible!" said Hollywood, backing up a few steps to take his customary hiding spot behind Resist.

"Who you calling horrible?" growled Troll. His voice sounded like a frozen yogurt machine attempting human speech.

"I resent that!" said Dare. HD TV really didn't do wonders for him or Click. You could see every matching blemish on their faces.

"It's bad enough we've had to hide in this junkyard out of shame," said Click. "We don't need any crap from the likes of you losers!"

"You no-good dirty rats!" said Mobster, his deep voice gone squeaky.

Motor shook his spray bottle, which magically changed the liquid inside from purple to red. "I know you don't want to hear this right now, but you've got to appreciate the poetic justice of all this."

"I'll be jitterbugged, you're right!" Hollywood said from behind Resist. "Ren Faire's always had a big head, and now it's literal!"

"I protest!" said Ren Faire.

Resist chuckled. "And Mobster's always passing the blame for his own shortcomings on 'dirty rats,' so it's only fitting he becomes one."

"You dirty—" Mobster started, then thought better of finishing the sentence.

"And Click and Dare are obsessed with being on-screen, so now they have their wish," I said. I must have looked intimidating in my wizard cloak, because they didn't talk back.

"And of course, Troll is always acting like a troll, and voilà, look at him now," said Motor.

Troll roared and charged straight at Motor.

And like that, whatever hopes we'd had of avoiding another Me rumble disappeared. I guess that had been wishful thinking anyway.

32

Viral Sensation

In the past, Troll could bring people to tears with his words alone. Now he had the muscles to match the power of his tongue.

Motor didn't seem too concerned, though. He lifted his spray bottle and took aim, shooting a powerful stream of red liquid straight into Troll's eyes. Screaming, Troll stumbled to his knees as he covered his monstrous face with his hands. Smoke billowed between his fingers. The other Virals stopped to help him.

"Prithee, what hast thou done?!" shouted Ren Faire, stooping over Troll.

"Yeah, I know that was self-defense, Motor, but it seems

like a low blow," said Hollywood. "Did you blind him or what?"

Motor, one of the gentlest Mes I knew, hardly looked bothered at all by the torture he'd just inflicted on Troll. If anything, he seemed excited. "Just watch," he said.

As if he had an emergency Off switch for pain, Troll stopped crying. He lifted his hands from his face to reveal that his monster features had disappeared. He was back to normal. At least, as normal as a Vulcan-eared jerk with a broken nose and a perma-scowl can ever be.

Troll and everyone else turned to Motor with the same look of bewilderment.

Motor held up the bottle so we could all see the label: CURSE REVERSE. "I actually wasn't sure if this stuff would work, since technically you were mutated, not cursed, but I figured it was worth a try. Anyway, I should have enough for all of you."

Troll touched his hands to his face again. With tears streaking down his cheeks, he struggled to get out two words he'd probably never said before in his life. "Th-thank you!"

Ren Faire hefted his massive eyebrows in confusion. "Prithee, why would you do this? Troll is thine enemy."

Motor shrugged. "You guys have been through enough. We all have. I mean, nobody deserves to be mutated and stuck someplace far from home, right?"

I might not have been as good a person as Motor, but the least I could do was back him up. "Guys, can we call a truce? We all have bigger problems than settling old scores."

The Rip crackled overhead.

"Speaking of bigger problems," said Meticulous from inside the bulb.

Though they barely looked like the rest of us anymore, the Virals all shook their heads in a very Me kind of way.

When Mobster unlocked the access panel on the giant lightbulb, Meticulous tumbled out of it and smacked to the ground.

"Thanks so much," said Meticulous, rubbing his back.

"Funny thing is, the bulb ain't even real!" said Mobster, giddy to have back his "regular old mug," as he called it.

"'Twas a marvelous prank!" said Ren Faire, moving his fingers all over his newly shrunken head as if to make sure it wouldn't blow up again.

Click twisted his fingers together in excitement. "I got a video of Meticulous screaming his head off when he thought we were really gonna fry him in that thing. Can't wait to post it when I'm online again. And then post my reaction video to it all."

Dare sighed. "I miss the internet."

Meticulous had kept his mouth shut as Motor cured the Virals and we filled them in on our mission. But the moment he got back on his feet, he headed toward the Stitch. I stepped in front of him to block his way. The old Meticulous would have shoved me aside and kept going. This new one wasn't so sure of his wrestling skills now that he knew they'd come from the fizz all along.

"Why'd you run out on us?" I asked.

Meticulous leaned over to smooth the wrinkles in his knickers. "I'm sorry, but the clock was ticking. I knew you'd be hemming and hawing and searching every inch of that revolting wizard's workshop. As far as I was concerned, I'd found what I needed, and that was enough. So I left."

"Jumpin' Jehoshaphat, that's cold!" said Hollywood.

"We definitely can't trust you now," said Motor.

"And how can we even be sure the Stitch is really what you say it is?" said Resist. "What if it's a weapon after all? It definitely looks like one."

Meticulous crossed his arms. "In less than two hours, by my calculations, the Rip will explode, bringing untold destruction in its wake. And then it won't matter who you trust and who you don't."

As if they'd been synchronized to the same clock, all the other Mes cleared their throats, ready to argue. We didn't have time for that. To get everybody's attention, I took off the cloak and let it fall to the ground. Ren Faire and Hollywood weren't the only ones around here with a sense of drama.

"I hate to admit it more than anybody else," I said. "But Meticulous is right. If we don't help him, all the people we love are dead."

Every Me in Mediocre Valley went from angry to surprised.

"You're all among the most intelligent Mes out there," I continued. This was a slight fib, since Click and Dare were in the audience. "All this time I've been with Meticulous, I've known he could just be conning me. Conning all of us. Maybe he still is."

Meticulous snorted.

"But at this point," I said, "all I can figure is that what I *know* Prez wants to do with the Rip is a lot worse than what Meticulous *claims* he wants to do with the Rip. Against my better judgment, my gut's telling me to trust Meticulous. And remember: we all have the same gut."

Nobody looked very convinced, and why should they? Meticulous had mistreated and abandoned Hollywood and the Viral Mes when they worked for him. He'd banished Resist from Me Con and crushed Motor's misguided belief in the goodness of all Mes. Considering how Meticulous had endangered my entire Earth, gotten me thrown in juvie, and shouted at me nonstop for the past day, I probably wasn't cut out to be a convincing advocate for him anyway.

Meticulous cleared his throat and fluffed out his coat-tails. "Thanks for the imagery, Average. When I look for someone to write my biography, I'll hit you up. Anyway, I'll spare you all a defense of my past actions. I won't even lecture you about the silliness of thinking in terms of 'good' or 'bad' when it comes to people. Instead, I'll simply ask you to help me correct this mistake I made. I'm not going to pretend I've changed. But maybe you'll consider changing how you feel about me. You don't have to like me; you just have to work with me. Thank you."

The other Mes almost looked convinced. Then Troll had to open his big mouth: "This whole stupid conversation is a moot point anyway!"

"And why is that?" I said.

"At yon hour, Prez and his plans are afoot!" said Ren Faire.

"What are you on about?" said Meticulous.

"I've hacked Prez's communications," said Troll. "He just announced he's going to start sending all the Mes home immediately."

I felt relieved and jealous at the same time. Unlike me, Prez had kept his promise to get the Mes home. He planned to finish the job I'd failed to do.

"Well, that's good, right?" said Hollywood. "All those Mes can get home. We can still shut down the Rip."

"It's not so simple," said Meticulous. "To make that many portals for that many Mes, he'll need to operate while the Rip is raging. It gives him more raw power to work with, and the barrier between worlds is thinner."

"So if we close the Rip, we save the multiverse," said Resist. "But we'll strand all those Mes here *again*."

"What sort of gosh-darned options are those?!" said Hollywood.

Troll pulled out his MePad. "That's not the worst of it." His screen showed a MeDrone's aerial view of the junkyard. It focused on the origami drive, and I got chills remembering what it was like to be stuck on that thing. Bolts from the Rip rained down all around the hunk of metal, but that didn't seem to bother the robotic soldiers standing beside it.

"Who are they?" I asked.

"They're just some of the alternate-Earth soldiers in Nash's Patchwork Platoon," said Click as the camera panned over the canyon. The place was crawling with soldiers of every possible flavor, from sandal-wearing Greeks to armor-plated cyborgs. They swarmed the junkyard and the outside of the HQ with the most bizarre assortment of tanks, cannons, and even a giant-robot mecha.

"*That's* the army Nash runs?" said Resist.

"He recruited any and every soldier who's been zapped to Earth Zero," said Dare.

"And he's mobilized them to round up all the Mes and take all their stuff," said Troll. "He's starting with the origami drive. He wants to see what makes it tick."

"Hence the storm," said Meticulous, watching a fresh batch of bolts clang across the sky.

Troll fiddled with the screen. "Nash would have raided Me HQ to round up the Mes by now too, but Twig is out there arguing that it's not legal. Take a look."

The camera zoomed in on another cliff overlooking the origami drive. Nash, in his general uniform, stood before Lunt, O'Fartly, and Pooplaski as they traded sharp words with Twig.

"She's only buying Prez a little time," I said. "If I know Nash and Lunt, they'll get their way soon enough. Prez will never have time to evacuate the Mes before the army busts in."

"And the longer the drive stays on, the worse the storm will get," said Motor.

"At this rate, we'll have very little time before the bloody Rip explodes for good," said Meticulous. "We can't fire the Stitch into the Rip when it's going bonkers like this. We need conditions as calm as possible." He moaned. "This is a shambles!"

"So we have to shut down the drive," I said. "And stop or slow the army so they don't reach Me HQ. Any suggestions?"

"You know," said Hollywood, "there was this episode of my old show, *Pallin' with the Shaolin*, where my character lit a keg of gunpowder to distract some guards so he could sneak into the prison and rescue his friends."

"What whimsy be this?!" said Ren Faire. "Mere distraction shan't stop those foul merchants of death!"

"No," said Resist, brightening. "But something else might. In all this junk you've passed by day after day, can you think of something we could use to blow up the drive? Something big, explosive, and mobile?"

The Viral Mes looked at each other and smiled.

"Mack," said Mobster. "We know just da thing!"

"Say we blow up the drive and stop the army," said Troll. "What then? We try to close the Rip? That means the Mes will be stuck here. And we'll *all* be stuck here. We don't have the right to make that choice for everybody."

Meticulous and I shared a glance, and just like with Motor, we didn't have to use any words. We had the same plan in mind.

"No, we don't have the right," I said. "But I'm gonna make the choice anyway. Because in this scenario, I'm the bad guy."

33

Flight of the *Titanic-Hindenburg*

All ten of us Mes had just climbed up to the roof of the flooded house when the air horn ripped through the sky like a point-blank tuba blast. Everybody jumped, which wasn't a safe thing to do on a pitched surface with loose shingles. Hollywood lost his balance and would have torpedoed off the gutters if Ren Faire hadn't grabbed him in time.

"Thanks!" Hollywood told his new pal as he got back on his feet.

"Prithee, comrade, mention it not!" Ren Faire said, slapping Hollywood's back.

In the half hour we'd spent getting our plan together and calling for a lift, Hollywood and Ren Faire had become good buddies. They'd put aside their old grudge with each other and bonded over theater stories. The same fuzzy spirit of friendship had brought together Motor and Troll, who traded hacker tips, and Mobster and Resist, who cracked each other up with their stories about telling off authority figures. Since everybody else was getting along with the Virals now, I probably should have forgiven Click and Dare for landing me in juvie. Instead, I took a page from Meticulous's book and ignored them. I figured if I really was a bad person, I might as well enjoy the perks of being a bad person: namely, ignoring people I didn't like.

Our new Viral allies had refused to tell us much of anything about the ship they'd called to pick us up. "You won't believe it until you see it," Troll had said. He'd been only partway right: even after I saw it, I *still* didn't believe it.

How do you make sense of a massive zeppelin carting an old-timey ocean liner beneath it? That's the monstrosity that, against all logic and reason, burst through the clouds and came barreling toward us. Letters on the side of its hull read: Titanic-Hindenburg.

"The *Titanic* and the *Hindenburg*?!" I said. "Combined?!"

Motor whistled low. "Two of the most famous crashes in history rolled into one."

"How can the balloon part even carry the boat part?" asked Hollywood.

"And who'd be moronic enough to fly in it?" said Resist.

"Motor! Average!" shouted two Mes from the deck of the ship. One wore the orange robes and serene expression of a

211

monk. The other looked tense, twitchy, and on the verge of a panic attack.

"Monk Me and Alien Abduction Me?!" I asked.

Ren Faire grinned. "Wait until thou doth see who's driving."

A third Me leaned his head out the window of the wheelhouse. He looked dashing with his brass-plated goggles, leather aviator helmet, and white scarf billowing in the wind.

"Gadzooks, if you'll pardon my language—that's Steampunk Me!" said Hollywood.

"All that talk about airships and steam technology, I figured he was making it up," said Resist.

"Steam technology," grumbled Meticulous. "What a joke."

Motor waved to Steampunk and the others. "Ahoy, Captain!"

Steampunk turned the steering wheel with one hand and clicked an impossible number of switches and levers with the other. Then he tugged on a droopy cable near his head, and the boat's smokestacks puffed thick white clouds of steam into the zeppelin above. The *Titanic-Hindenburg* floated toward us.

"When did that swot get so . . . adequate?" said Meticulous.

"He's not just adequate," said Hollywood as Steampunk stopped the ship just above the roof. "He's cool!"

Monk and Alien Abduction lowered a rope ladder so we could all climb up to the deck. Once we got aboard, Steampunk pointed the ship to float farther down the canyon. Then he stepped out of the wheelhouse to join his crew, giving every Me a crisp salute, until he saw Meticulous and his floating Stitch.

"What are you doing here with *him*?!" said Steampunk.

Alien Abduction raised his fists at Meticulous. "He must have you all under mind control!" yelled the paranoid Me. "We have to stop him!"

Monk patted Alien Abduction on the shoulder. "Now, now. Clearly, the multiverse has brought them together," said Monk. "And now it has brought us all together." Monk motioned toward three more Mes working machinery in the background: Rodeo Clown Me, Sensitive Me, and Disco Me. They looked even less happy to see Meticulous than the others did, which made sense, considering that Meticulous had stranded them here longer than any other Me. Sensitive mumbled a slew of angry words that came out muffled by the filter mask. I figured we were better off not hearing them.

Ignoring him, I turned to Steampunk. "Well, this is a fine ship you've got here."

Steampunk swept his eyes over the monstrosity with a loving look. "Everybody thought I was lying about coming from a steampunk world, but there's the proof. The *Titanic-Hindenburg* is the most famous airship from my

Earth. The ultimate in advanced steam technology. It went missing after its first flight. To think it wound up here, and I found it!"

Meticulous watched a swarm of sea gulls in tuxedoes flying past. "It shouldn't fly, but somehow, against all logic and reason . . . it does."

"Logic and reason are not the only forces at play in the multiverse," said Monk.

Meticulous had a counterargument for that claim, but I cut him off. "And Troll filled you in on our plan when he contacted you, right, Steampunk?" I said. "You're okay with . . . what we have in mind?"

Steampunk sighed. "It won't be easy, but if it means stopping Prez and his stupid plans to exploit the Rip, then it'll be worth it."

"I don't trust Prez for a second!" said Alien Abduction. "My theory is that he's in league with the aliens who took me!"

"But we don't need to hear the details of that theory at this time," said Monk. "Believe me, we've heard much of it these many weeks."

"Well then," I said. "Set a course for the origami drive. It's time we take the fight to Nash's army!"

And to my surprise, every Me on the deck of the *Titanic-Hindenburg* cheered. Despite everything I'd done, it was almost like they saw me as some kind of leader. Hopefully, I wasn't leading them to disaster.

Steampunk piloted his impossible ship out of the canyon and up over Nash's army. Before the soldiers had a chance to fire their weapons on us, we doused them in the most powerful magic the Polymagic Vocational Institute had to offer.

The army didn't stand a chance.

Before the ship had arrived, Motor, Meticulous, and I had spent our time folding origamagic bombs from Motor's backpack stash of blank scroll paper and spell books. Now we sent it all raining down on the troops. The Winston's Wand Whirler spun soldiers around until they were too dizzy to stand. The Morton's Mop Monsters tangled up the tanks. And some well-placed Never-Stop Ghost Hammers, Artificial Elf Cobblers, and Metal-Melting Dragon Tongues took out the cannons, robots, and other machinery of war. Most satisfying of all, a swarm of Sylvania's Soaring Sponges chased away General Nash and Council Members Lunt, Pooplaski, and O'Fartly.

Through it all, my MeMinder never once told me I was being bad, so I figured I must have been onto something.

When the ship pulled within range of the origami drive, a red-alert siren blared. Then the ship began its downward collision course with the giant dish of doom.

"Get to your assigned bat bikes, people!" shouted Steampunk.

He pointed us toward a stack of bikes latched along the

sides of the deck. They came equipped with small steam engines and big mechanical bat wings.

"I still don't like this," moaned Hollywood. Every Me but Steampunk grabbed a bike and hopped on.

"We've got no choice," said Resist. As soon as she started pedaling, the bike's steam engine kicked in and the wings started to flap. It looked ludicrous, but it worked. Resist rose up over the deck and off the side, flapping her way toward the nearest cliff.

The rest of us followed suit, except for Motor, who hopped onto his flying carpet, and Steampunk, who stayed behind as long as he could. Craning my neck as I rose into the clouds, I watched Steampunk stand at the prow of the ship, arms raised to the sky as he shouted, "I'm king of the world!"

He waited until the last possible second to leave the ship on a souped-up bat bike with double wings and a big steam engine. Riding that thing, he caught up to us in no time.

"She was a real beauty of a ship!" I yelled to Steampunk as he pulled up alongside me.

Steampunk choked back tears. "I know that with a name like *Titanic-Hindenburg*, she was fated to sink someday anyway. She might as well have gone down for a good cause, in a blaze of glory."

We turned back around just in time to see the ship hit its target.

Imagine a chalkboard the size of a JumboTron getting scratched by the fingernails of the Jolly Green Giant. That's what it sounded like when the *Titanic-Hindenburg* crashed into the origami drive. The noise vibrated the very blood cells in my bones.

The Rip let loose with three lightning strikes in a row. They struck the canyon below, launching a miniature avalanche of transdimensional garbage. Soldiers scrambled around, and Nash, from the safety of a cliff, shouted at them to take cover.

Hollywood crouched down on his bat bike, swiveling his head around to see where the next strike would come from. "Uh, wasn't that storm supposed to calm down after we broke the origami drive?"

"Maybe the Rip's too far gone," said Resist.

Meticulous gazed at the growing hole in the sky as we pedaled toward Me HQ and the common yard came into view. "The Rip is going critical. We'll have to work double time once we get down there." He turned to me. "Just keep them distracted as long as you can."

"Good luck," I said.

He nodded as he banked his bike toward the missile launcher below. The Virals and the former crew of the *Titanic-Hindenburg* followed him. Seconds later, they blinked out of sight. Resist had shared with them a new line of Me Corp. products she'd been developing—CoverMe InvisiRings and InvisiCloaks. The Mes wore the rings, and they'd draped a cloak over the Stitch, hauling it alongside their bikes, which had also disappeared from view.

"Isn't it dangerous to sell invisibility rings to the general public?" asked Hollywood.

"I don't plan to sell them," said Resist. "I plan to donate them to refugees, political protesters, and other people who need a leg up against authority figures. I only wish the effect lasted longer. Once the battery wears out, no more invisibility."

"Hopefully, it'll last long enough for us to launch the Stitch undetected," said Motor.

"And if not, well, we'll have to be even more distracting down there," I said. "So let's go pay a visit to Prez."

34

Please Release Me

Any large gathering of my counterparts always seemed to end in me getting chased down by an angry mob or covered in Godzilla snot. That's why it came as such a shock to be not just welcomed at the Me party to end all Me parties, but to be the guest of honor.

When Motor, Resist, Hollywood, and I stepped into the lounge at Me HQ, every Me on the dance floor screamed for us like we were some kind of K-pop boy band. It felt even better than throwing a ball of dung at Nash's face.

"We saw what you did out there in that crazy ship!" said Pool Hustler Me, pointing to the big screen near the ceiling. It showed an aerial view of Nash's army in tatters.

"Excellent strategy!" yelled Military School Me, giving me a salute.

Up onstage, Bollywood Musical Me yelled into his mic. "This next number's dedicated to the Mes who saved us!" He and the Tune Mes broke into a song that had been stuck in my head for the past three months. Given how loudly everybody groaned, it must have been stuck in their heads all this time too.

Across the room, I saw Prez waving us over. He sat at a long cafeteria table beside Juvenile Hall, who tapped away at his MePad with furious speed. Cowboy and Acupuncture stood over them, keeping a watchful eye on everyone.

We made our way through the crowd to reach them but had to stop for so many selfies and fist bumps along the way that it took forever. By the time we reached the table, Juvenile Hall had made a few final taps on the screen and proclaimed, "Done!" He unplugged a familiar sleek MeMinder from his MePad and handed it to Prez. "The portals should work now with no problem. Sorry for the hiccups, daddy-o."

Prez strapped on the watch and powered it up. "Perfectly understandable." He nodded at us. "Excellent work, you four. We saw the whole thing on the drone camera feed. You did us a great service out there."

"Yeah, you're really some cool cats!" said Juvenile Hall. "Sorry again for throwing you into the origami drive."

"I suppose we returned the favor,

didn't we?" said Resist. "By vaporizing your dangerous toy?"

I cringed on the inside. Resist had been away from other humans too long to remember how to play nice. We had to butter up Prez so he'd stay distracted, at least long enough to buy Meticulous some time.

Rather than blow up, Prez chuckled. "Actually, you wrecking the origami drive did us another big favor. It keeps the thing out of the council's hands."

"But it cost you control of the Rip," said Motor. "That doesn't upset you?"

"Why should it?" said Prez, pressing the screen of his watch. "Now I have this."

Green light beamed from the watch, making a portal in the air ahead of him.

"Even more good news, people!" Prez announced to the crowd. "Not only did Average and his friends stop the army that was coming for us, but my MeMinder, powered by Average's mojo, is up and running again! That means we can start cranking out the gateways to get you all home!"

The Mes went delirious. The music and dancing stopped as everyone jostled to get a place in line. For a second there I worried about another Me rumble breaking out, but Prez was on top of it. "Whoa there, let's chill!" he said. "Juvenile Hall preprogrammed the MeMinder to generate all your portals in a set order, and we have the processing power to do only one at a time. So, who's from Earth One Hundred Fourteen? You're up first!"

As Prez consulted with Juvenile Hall, Hollywood lowered his voice to a whisper. "Prez doesn't seem like such a bad guy," he said. "And he's got great fashion sense."

"Don't you see, he's automatically a bad guy," said Resist. "He's a politician!"

"But he's sending the Mes back, like he promised," said Motor. "He's keeping his word."

Unlike me. Why did I still feel inferior to Prez, even when I knew he was dead wrong about the Rip?

A Me I'd never seen before stepped up to Prez. He had messy hair and wild eyes that darted around like he expected something to jump out at any moment. He looked frightened as Acupuncture handed him two bags full of equipment.

"That cat is Post-Apocalypse Me," Juvenile Hall whispered to us. "From Earth One Hundred Fourteen. You wound up in his house when you showed up here."

"You were tracking us?" I asked.

"Of course they were," muttered Resist. "This is a surveillance state!"

Prez gave Post-Apocalypse a sad smile.  "You've got a hard road ahead, but hopefully the equipment in those bags will help you get your Earth back on track."

Post-Apocalypse's lower lip trembled. "Th-thank you. For everything!"

"Of course, my brother," said Prez, giving him an elbow tap.

Taking a deep breath, Post-Apocalypse strapped on a gas mask from his bag and walked into the portal.

Prez shook his head. "That poor Me. Life won't be easy. But thanks to you, Average, lending us your fizz and slowing down that army, he has a chance. Do you know how much technology I sent with Post-Apocalypse? We gave him the full package."

Hollywood pulled a flash drive from his pocket. "I have some copies of my old show, *Baker's Dozen,* here. Maybe we could throw those in there as a bonus gift for the next Mes who leave?"

Prez beamed at him. "Perfect!" He took the drive and tossed it to Juvenile Hall. "Copy these, will you? And see that everyone gets a copy on their way out of here."

Hollywood nudged Resist in the ribs. "See, he's not as bad as you thought!"

Resist glared at him until he stepped away from her.

"I'm glad everybody will get to help their worlds with the stuff you got from other Earths," I told Prez. "But let's not forget that there won't be *any* Earths if you don't let us fix the Rip."

"You know I can't do that," said Prez. "We're doing too much good here." He started tapping at his MeMinder again to make another portal.

"But Nash and his army, plus the council, will eventually make their way here," I said. "What if you can't get everybody out in time? Or if you all end up as fugitives?"

"It will have been worth it to get you all home," said

Prez. "So go ahead and take your spot in line. We'll send you home too."

For just a fleeting second, I was tempted. The portal I'd made to get here could have been a fluke. Even if I could repeat the process, I'd need a lot more practice and a lot more fizz, two things in short supply at the moment. Why not just leave all this behind and forget about the Rip? Wasn't that what rotten people like me did?

But I figured even rotten people deserved to have a home to come back to, and that meant staying here to fix the Rip.

"Okay, clearly we can't talk you out of it, so I'll cut to the chase," I said. "We propose a challenge."

Prez looked up from the MeMinder screen, intrigued. "Oh?"

"We know how much you like challenges," said Resist.

"So here's what we propose," I said. "We win, you let us fix the Rip. You win, you get to keep on using the Rip however you like."

Prez's MeMinder shot out another portal. "Earth Ninety-Four!" he called.

Lucha Libre high-fived everybody on his way through the crowd on a victory lap. Acupuncture handed him a bag of wonders, and Prez gave him a curtsy before he stepped through.

"I like to use the local form of farewell for each of my brother Mes," he

explained to us. "Now, about your offer. We have a lot of portals to get through."

"You can set your MeMinder to auto," said Resist.

"True, daddy-o," said Juvenile Hall. "I can manage for you. And I'll be close by in case something comes up."

"So, do you accept?" I said.

In answer, Prez took off his MeMinder and tossed it to Juvenile Hall. "We never back down from a challenge on Earth Zero. There's just one thing."

"Yeah?" I said.

"Let's do it outside," said Prez. "That way I can keep a better eye on Meticulous and his invisible friends who've been sneaking around the missile launcher out there."

35

Make 'Em Laugh

It seemed only fitting that yet again, I'd been busted by a MeMinder.

The advanced scanning equipment built into Prez's MeMinder had detected Meticulous and his team of Mes at the missile launcher. The CoverMe rings had begun to wear off anyway, and the Mes started reappearing in pieces: the ruffles of Meticulous's shirt, Ren Faire's ponytail, Troll's pointy ears, Mobster's pin-striped butt. That's how we found them when we filed outside.

"I was so close!" Meticulous said as Acupuncture and Cowboy pulled him out of the Stitch. He'd stuffed himself into a full-size compartment within the device. I hadn't even realized there'd been room for a person in there.

Meticulous recognized my confusion. "It's bigger on the inside," he said as Acupuncture brought him over to us. "One of the magical modifications None of Me made."

"Don't worry," Prez said. "We'll leave this impressive piece of technology on the launcher in case you and your team win."

Cowboy and Acupuncture laughed like that would never happen. Behind them, Juvenile Hall adjusted Prez's Me-Minder until it popped out a portal for Pool Hustler, who darted through with his parting gift of revolutionary technology.

The Rip raged overhead, but that was nothing compared to the major hissy fit brewing behind Meticulous's eyes. "See how bad that is?" he screamed to Prez. "It's gotten worse, not better! You *need* to let me fix it!"

Prez looked at the sky, and I thought I saw a trace of doubt cross his face. Then it passed and he smiled again. That's when I realized the truth about Prez. He wasn't bad. He probably even wanted to be good. But what he wanted above all else was to believe in the lies he told himself.

"It'll calm down soon enough," said Prez.

"It always does. Teams of five, people. Cowboy, Average, you're with me. Plus Bollywood Musical and Kabuki Theater, since you're in the back of the line anyway. Average, choose your group from the batch you came with."

It wasn't hard to pick my first three team members: Resist, Motor, and Hollywood were natural choices. But choosing from the lineup of other Mes was as awkward as having to pick a lab partner at school. I knew I had to go with Meticulous so we could modify our plan now that he'd been busted. But how could we function as a team with the least team-minded Me of all?

As Juvenile Hall called up more Mes to send home, Prez pulled his group into a huddle. I did the same.

"I was so close," said Meticulous, taking his place beside me.

"Why were you inside the Stitch, anyway?" I asked. "I thought you were just supposed to launch it."

Meticulous wouldn't meet my eyes. "Oh, just some final adjustments."

"You're lying," I said. "I can tell. The Stitch needs a pilot, doesn't it?"

"Keep it down!" said Meticulous, glancing over his shoulder. "The Stitch is a tool to fix the Rip, but it has no brain. Not even I could do the programming it would need to function on its own, and there's too much interference to do it by remote control. Somebody's got to go up there in the Rip to do the calculations on the spot. Someone with an intimate understanding of the multi-verse, genius-level math skills, and nerves of steel."

Hollywood did a little dance, waving ta-da hands in the air. "That would be me!"

"Dude, not the best time for a joke," said Resist.

Hollywood's face fell. "I didn't think he was serious. You're *really* going up there?!"

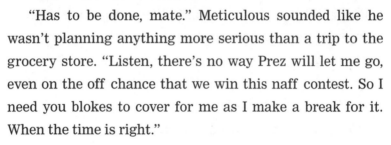

"That's suicide!" said Motor.

"Has to be done, mate." Meticulous sounded like he wasn't planning anything more serious than a trip to the grocery store. "Listen, there's no way Prez will let me go, even on the off chance that we win this naff contest. So I need you blokes to cover for me as I make a break for it. When the time is right."

At the edge of the common yard, Juvenile Hall made steady progress getting the line of Mes into their portals home. There must have been sixty left by now, not including the fifteen or so Mes we'd brought along when we'd crashed the party. Above, the Rip raged. Nash was surely gathering his army. At this rate, against these odds, Prez would never get everybody home in time.

"Okay, we're ready," Prez announced. "I think the Remember Me Challenge will be the most fitting today!"

The line of Mes cheered.

"For the new folks, it's simple," continued Prez. "We

draw from a list of key childhood memories that all of us share. Then the two teams act it out. The crowd favorite wins. Let's get ready!"

"By the way," said Meticulous. "I nominate my *former* assistant as team captain."

"Yeah, real funny!" said Hollywood.

"I'm serious," said Meticulous. "You know acting."

"Totally!" I said.

Hollywood looked for confirmation from Resist and Motor, who didn't hesitate to agree.

"I won't let you down!" said Hollywood, getting weepy.

"Oh please," said Resist. "Don't make me regret agreeing to this."

From the audience, Ren Faire shouted, "Huzzah, Hollywood! Thou shalt prevail!"

Hollywood slammed his fist into his tender palm and didn't even wince. "Let's do this!" he said.

Aqua Aerobics Me stepped between the two teams and pulled a slip from the wads of paper in his swim cap. "The first memory is: 'Saying Goodbye to Mom and Dad on the First Day of Kindergarten.' Go!"

With scary precision, Prez's team assumed their roles and took their spots for the scene. Cowboy as the teacher, Acupuncture as the assistant teacher, Kabuki Theater as Dad, and Bollywood Musical as Mom. Prez played the six-year-old version of us, throwing himself into the role, tears and all. "I don't wanna go!" he cried. We all remembered shouting those exact words, and he captured all the fear and pain and embarrassment that went behind them. Every Me on the field who was watching started crying, including us.

"How are we gonna compete with that?" Resist said between sniffles.

Wiping away his tears, Hollywood sized up the lawn before us like a coach looking over a playing field. "We can't compete, but we don't have to. Just follow my lead."

He assigned us our parts and we took the lawn-stage. As Young Meade, Hollywood started bawling, but he went way overboard into tantrum territory, throwing himself on the ground and kicking his legs. A few Mes chuckled.

"This is a shambles!" Meticulous whispered to me. "Get ready. I'll make a run for it."

After writhing around some more, Hollywood lifted his head and turned to the audience. Everyone expected to hear "I don't wanna go." Instead, they got: "I think I peed my pants!"

The crowd erupted in laughter. Even Prez and his team cracked up. Ren Faire started clapping, and soon every Me joined in. Hollywood invited us to take a bow with him.

"I guess comedy's not so bad after all," Hollywood whispered to us.

As the laughter died down, Aqua Aerobics returned to the spot between our teams. "We've polled the audience and the results are in. We have a tie!"

"Well done!" said Prez. "Let's draw again and try another."

"Or not!" shouted Meticulous. "You really think we should be wasting our time with the 'Third-Grade Spelling Bee Humiliation,' the 'Full-Body Poison Ivy Disgrace,' or the 'Barfing on the Dental Hygienist Fiasco'? The fate of entire Earths is at stake!"

As if to help make his case, the Rip filled the whole sky now, blasting lightning all over the place.

"Actually," Hollywood whispered, "I have some killer ideas for the 'Barfing on the Dental Hygienist Fiasco.'"

Everyone else went quiet as Prez thought things over. The only sound beyond the thunder was the pop of portals as Mes made their way through the line.

Finally, Prez spoke. "I still say the Rip will calm down soon enough. But since Meticulous is so obviously waiting for a chance to make a break for it and launch his device, let's settle this now. I propose something more definitive: the OrigaME Challenge. One of you goes up against me. The best origami wins."

The rest of the team nodded at me, including Meticulous. Suddenly, I felt a little less bad about myself.

"Okay then, I accept," I said.

"Good!" said Prez. He turned to Juvenile Hall. "My Me-Minder, please? Sorry, everyone, I'll just need it a moment, and then we can get back to the portals."

Juvenile Hall tossed him the watch, which Prez slipped back onto his wrist.

"Let's have a seat, then."

Prez used his MeMinder to summon a sheet of 3-D printer paper, which he folded into a small round table and two padded chairs in no time flat.

If he was trying to intimidate me before an origami-folding contest, then mission accomplished.

36

A Stitch in Time

I took a seat at the origami table Prez had made for our origami duel. It might have been comfortable if I hadn't resented him for being able to fold it in the first place.

"Now, then," said Prez, pulling a sheet of crisp, clean paper from the stack that Pool Hustler Me brought him. "The idea of the OrigaME Challenge is we fold something near and dear to all Mes."

I nodded, running my fingers over my sheet to get a feel for the paper.

We waited for the signal from Pool Hustler, then got to folding. Right out of the gate, Prez whipped together a perfect paper replica of Mr. Fartz—the beloved stuffed-toy version, not the creepy devil assistant version.

"Nice!" I said. And I meant it. His rapid-fire fingers had moved so quickly, I'd totally missed how he'd done it. He had better origami skills than I did, and he might even have been able to fold an ouroboros if he'd put his mind to it. None of the origami in my repertoire could compare to his take on Mr. Fartz. But then, they didn't have to. I'd chosen to make the most familiar origami I knew, and I'd finished it with ease.

In front of Prez I placed an origami octopus, no better or worse than the others I'd made over the years.

"Looks great," said Prez, with the grace of a winner. "But I'm not so sure it meets the criteria of a thing all Mes love. We can put it to a vote, but I'm afraid this might just disqualify you."

"That's cool," I said. "I wasn't playing to win."

And that's when the octopus came alive. I'd switched out Pool Hustler's parchment for the last piece of scroll paper from Meticulous's stash. Everyone screamed as the creature quadrupled in size and slid across the table to wrap its long, wriggling arms around Prez.

"Now!" I said.

Meticulous bolted for the Stitch as my friends sprang into action. Resist charged at Cowboy; Hollywood went after Acupuncture. Motor hung back, drawing runes on his MePad as he muttered an incantation over the screen.

I reached across the table for Prez's MeMinder, hoping to tear it off his wrist. But even engulfed in the arms of an octopus, Prez managed to switch on his MeMinder's 3-D origami printer. He folded himself a giant pair of scissors. With a few well-placed snips, my octopus fell apart in a pile of lifeless confetti. It didn't matter—Meticulous had made it to the Stitch and hopped inside.

With just a few more taps and some fast folding, Prez made a giant falcon that flew from his hands, growing in size as it sped toward the Stitch. Swooping down, it snatched Meticulous out of the Stitch by his shoulders and hauled him upward. Meticulous raged, squirming so hard that he fell from the bird's talons and plopped on the ground, passing out cold.

The Mes in line grumbled. If they were like me—and they were—the Mes didn't enjoy seeing any of us treated this way. The flashing bolts shooting down from the Rip didn't do much to ease their concern either.

"Not cool!" said Juvenile Hall. Acupuncture and Cowboy nodded in agreement.

Prez called for silence, but nobody listened, so he had to stand up and raise his voice even higher. "Everyone, please, this was an unfortunate mistake! Now, let's everybody line up, and I'll get some more portals going. Remember, one at a time. It's all my processor can take."

Lightning struck the spot just in front of Prez, knocking him off his feet. Mes started to panic, running all over the place. Above, the Rip looked ready to tear the sky in half.

"Motor!" I yelled over the storm. "Whatever you're planning, now's the time!"

Nodding, Motor drew the final rune on his screen and said his last incantation. A white light beamed from his screen straight to my MeMinder X. The watch shuddered on my wrist as a glowing hologram popped out. It was Dad, or at least some weird robotic version of Dad. With a blank, emotion-free face, he looked from the Rip raging above to Prez's MeMinder. "This is not a good deed," he said.

Robo-Dad flew straight at Prez, who'd just sat up. The Me barely had time to flinch as Robo-Dad disappeared inside his MeMinder.

"You brought the Good Deed Tracker to life!?" I yelled to Motor.

"Not exactly," Motor yelled back. "Mostly I just gave it more responsibility!"

"This is *not* a good deed!" yelled Prez's watch. A monsoon of transdimensional goop blasted from the device and ricocheted all over the common.

As the goop bounced around, it left behind little swirls of glowing energy beside every Me. The whirlpools of green light stretched until they grew big enough for each Me to fit through. The hacked MeMinder had made everyone a personal portal home.

A doorway opened beside me too, and I saw my room on the other side. My real room, from my Earth. Just a few steps and I could go back.

"Get out of here before the Rip explodes!" yelled Motor.

He didn't have to tell my doubles twice. As bolts of lightning struck the ground around them, the Mes skedaddled through the doorways back to their Earths. Alien Abduction, Monk, Steampunk, Juvenile Hall, the Virals, and all the rest disappeared, their portals blinking shut behind them. Acupuncture and Cowboy paused at their portals, looking to Prez for direction. As a resident of Earth Zero, Prez had no other place to go. He was stuck here without a portal of his own.

Over by the launcher, Meticulous lay in the light of his portal, still passed out. I could tell that Motor, Hollywood, and Resist wanted to leave, by the hungry way they stared into their portals. But they waited to see what I'd do.

Prez and I jinxed each other as we yelled the same words to our friends: "Leave! I'll be fine!"

With a salute, the Secret Service Mes made for their exits.

My three friends weren't so quick to vamoose. They stood in front of their portals, gesturing for me to step through mine.

"It's too late to fix the Rip!" Motor screamed. "Leave! Maybe we can survive!"

"Don't get any ideas about throwing your life away!" said Resist. "That piece of junk Meticulous made probably won't even work!"

"Come on!" said Hollywood. "We did what we could!"

They might have said more, but out of nowhere, a glowing green hand appeared in front of each of them and pushed them into their portals. Once they'd stumbled through, the portals popped into nothingness.

My eyes followed the hands as they flew back into Prez's MeMinder.

"You were right!" Prez shouted to me. "The Rip is out of control! I figured you'd never talk your friends into leaving, so I helped them along. I also figure I can't convince you to go home either!" He nodded toward Meticulous. "But I can give you cover!"

Prez produced another sheet of glowing green paper and folded it into a lightning rod. He shoved it into the ground, then rolled away just as it drew the latest bolt from the Rip. More lightning struck at the rod, drawing the worst of the storm away from the spot where Meticulous lay.

"It won't last long!" Prez yelled.

Giving him a nod of thanks, I ran for Meticulous. When I reached him, I tried shaking him awake, but he was out cold. I toyed with the idea of slapping him, which would have been more satisfying, but even if I woke him up, he'd still be too groggy to operate the Stitch.

That left only one option.

I ran for the launcher.

I'd barely started when I heard  Meticulous chasing after me.

"You're in no shape to go!" I called to him.

"Like you are?!" he yelled back.

He somehow pulled ahead of me

239

and reached the missile launcher first. As he scrambled up and mounted the Stitch, I followed right behind him.

"No, *I'm* doing this!" I grabbed him by the shoulders.

Meticulous tried to tear my hands away, but I held on tight.

"Isn't this a rather extreme way to prove to yourself that you're not *bad*?" he grunted.

"Like you haven't been doing the same all this time?" I said.

I yanked Meticulous backward just as he heaved himself forward, and somehow we tumbled into the machine together.

Slamming into the compartment in a tangle with Meticulous, I learned firsthand that the contraption really *was* bigger on the inside. As the Stitch shot into the sky, I could take comfort in the knowledge that although we might have been hurtling toward certain death, at least there was room for two.

37

You and Me Both

Like a toddler refusing to take medicine, the Rip did its best to keep Meticulous and me from getting in. The storm pulverized us and our flying coffin of a ride as we barreled through the pinball-machine sky.

I knew we might get crushed or ripped apart at any moment. I could even accept that we might die very, very soon. I just wished I'd had more time. Time to see Mom and Dad again. Time to tell Twig how I really felt about her. Time to say goodbye to Motor, Hollywood, Resist, and all the other Mes. Even the ones I didn't like very much.

"You're wishing you could have said goodbye," said Meticulous, removing his leg from my rib.

"When did you get so good at reading Mes?" I said, lifting my elbow from his stomach.

"Lots of time to reflect when I was stranded on that horrible, awful Earth where you left me."

"You're bringing that up again?"

"And I always will." I could tell he was smiling, even if I couldn't see it.

We had no view window to see the Rip, but I knew we were getting closer, because the fizz came back, hotter than ever. So much energy poured into me that I could have burst out of the metal cocoon with nothing but a flex of my arms.

"I can feel it again," I said. "The fizz."

"Me too," said Meticulous. "I never thought I'd admit this, but it's . . . invigorating. I can see why you rely on it so much. I'd become a lazy incompetent just like you if I let myself rely on this crutch."

I laughed.

The shaking stopped all at once, and for a peaceful moment, we flew straight and calm.

"Eye of the storm!" said Meticulous. "We made it inside the Rip!"

After what we'd gone through to get there, I would have expected to end our flight with an epic crash landing. Instead, the Stitch just sort of stopped with a soft thunk.

And sat there.

"Did we just land?" I asked. "Aren't we in the sky?"

"We're in the Rip," said Meticulous. "It's not the sky; it's not the land. It's sort of in between, or inside out. Basically, you'll just have to see for yourself."

"Can we breathe out there?"

Meticulous scowled. "This is where the manky magic comes in. A feature None of Me added. I don't approve, but I didn't have time to think up a scientific approach."

The Stitch started to bend and buckle like a soda can getting stepped on. I panicked all over again as the metal shell collapsed around our bodies. My brain managed to think past the fear and adrenaline just enough to realize this wasn't any random flattening. The metal was foil-wrapping around me on purpose, like it had been preprogrammed to do this. In moments, what I'd figured would be my coffin changed into a suit of armor that fit me like a glove.

A clear faceplate formed in front of my eyes, letting me see the inside of the Rip.

We stood in an endless chamber made from clear green goop. It was like being stuck inside a bottle of Fierce Green Apple Gatorade. The floor, walls, and ceiling of the chamber were just clear enough to show a view outside like nothing even a video game designer could have dreamed up. Hundreds of Earths floated all around us, exact copies of the same planet drifting along at the dead pace of three-day-old birthday balloons. Every so often, one of these Earths would crash into another, and a hole would open in the floor, spraying a fountain of fire and sparks that usually sputtered out after a few seconds. Some of these eruptions didn't stop, and others looked as large and steady as geysers that wouldn't run out anytime soon.

"Welcome to the crawl space of the multiverse," said Meticulous. He wore a Stitch suit of his own. "The broken buffer between Earths. The Rip."

"Stop being such a goof," I said. I'd never admit it to him, but I'd grown to enjoy his flair for drama. "So what's up with those geysers?"

"That's what we're here to fix. They're the ruptures that have been forming at a growing rate these past months."

He pointed to a nearby geyser so large that the goop shot from it in thick ribbons that danced in the air.

"How do we fix *that*?!" I said. "And all the others. There must be dozens!"

"Hundreds," said Meticulous. "It's bad, but not as bad as it looks. They're all connected, just like the Earths around us are connected. So in theory, if we fix a few of the bigger ones, the others should more or less follow their lead and fix themselves too. It's all in how we fold them."

"Fold? As in, origami?"

"What else?" he said, heading toward the nearest rupture. He waved for me to follow.

Moving through the Rip felt like walking along the deep end of a swimming pool. A smaller geyser popped up at our side, and the blast sent me stumbling. I stopped myself just before falling headfirst into the rupture. Up close, I could see patterns in the green energy spilling out of it. They broke apart and merged together and spun around in an endless dance. The longer I looked, the more I thought I saw little origami folds inside them. "It's beautiful!" I said.

"Quite," said Meticulous. "Has your digital display kicked in?"

As soon as he said this, my faceplate lit up. A MePad interface framed its edges with a menu bar.

"Activate the Automatic Origami Folding Array command," said Meticulous.

I saw the command in the menu and blinked at it. Something clicked in the suit, and I felt the chest plate unfold and re-form into a small cannon barrel. Meticulous's suit did the same. FOLDING ARRAY ENABLED flashed on my screen.

"Point it at the rupture!" said Meticulous. "Hurry! It's about to blow!"

Just as we swiveled the barrels at the flailing ribbons of goop, more energy than ever blasted from the rupture, knocking us back. The geysers all around us rose even higher and the floor shook. A message on the display read ORIGAMI ARRAY MALFUNCTION, followed by RIP DESTRUCTION IMMINENT.

I looked around for Meticulous but didn't see him anywhere. I screamed his name as the geyser before me grew higher and higher.

With no real idea what I was supposed to be doing, I reached out and grabbed the ribbons wriggling from the rupture. They were as wide and as flat as paper, so I did what came naturally to me.

I folded them.

38

Get Me Outta Here

Folding the rupture was like trying to wrestle a gang of inflatable floppy balloon men during a hurricane. The whipping tentacles of energy bucked in my hands, ready to slip away any second. But with more fizz in me than ever, I managed to hold on.

Meticulous appeared at my side, looking dumbstruck through his faceplate. "I don't believe it!" he said.

"Where did you go?" I asked.

He pointed to a cluster of Earths behind him. "I got hoofed all the way over there. Need a hand?"

I held down the folded flaps, which kept jumping around

in my hands, eager to break free. "Sure. What sort of fold were these doohickeys going to make?"

"A combination of at least twenty, and that's just to start. That's why the origami array would have come in handy."

"We have to fold this twenty more times?!"

"And the next rupture may need different folds altogether. There's no single perfect fold that will fix everything."

My brain nearly melted from the lightbulb that turned on inside it. I twisted the flaps in my hands to start a new fold. "There *is* a fold that might just fix everything. That's what he was trying to tell us with that note."

"What are you on about?" said Meticulous. He caught on the next moment. "The ouroboros? But it's the Impossible Fold!"

"Yeah, and we're in an impossible situation. What have we got to lose?"

It took everything Meticulous and I had learned about origami in all our thirteen years. It took his genius-level math. It took my imagination. It took every skill and mental power of every Me that we could both borrow through the fizz.

But together, we did it. We turned a cosmic tear into an ouroboros, the Impossible Fold that fed into itself.

The rupture sealed over like it had never come apart. Then the ruptures all around stopped spewing their ribbons of energy, and soon enough they sealed up too. And just like that, the Rip wasn't a Rip anymore.

My head fizzed, and I saw a vision of Earth Zero in my brain. The Rip disappeared from the sky, and with it, all the people, creatures, buildings, and other stuff that didn't belong there. I saw Prez and the Twig of his Earth holding hands as they watched the junkyard of the multiverse turn back into an empty canyon again. A perfectly lovely canyon.

"It's working!" I told Meticulous. "I can see it working."

We turned to each other and almost made the motion to hug. Then we thought better of it.

"Listen, what you did—" I started.

"What *we* did."

"Always correcting me." I smiled. "That's just one of the reasons it's been horrible being with you these past few days."

He grinned back. "I just realized we're even now. You trapped me on a prehistoric Earth, and now I've trapped you here. Guess I've really shown you up."

We laughed, but it got old fast as the realization sank in: there was no escape from this place, a place that wouldn't even exist in a few moments.

Then a hand punched through the floor of the Rip, followed by an arm and a head. A hooded head.

"None of Me?" Meticulous and I said together.

The dark wizard Me pulled himself all the way out of the hole and stood before us, his black cloak swirling around, even though there wasn't any wind. He reached for his hood to pull it off. I don't know what I'd been expecting. Scars? Green lizard scales? Extreme tattoos and piercings?

Nope. When the hood came away, he looked just like us.

"You know, you're the first actual Mes I've met in person," he said in a perfectly normal Me voice. The hole he'd just busted through covered back over like it had never been there.

"What were you doing, uh, down there?" I said.

"I wasn't exactly down there, more like *all around* this place." He cringed. "It was gross. I came here to slow the Rip's spread and got stuck. It was kind of like leaning too far over to fix a car engine and getting trapped under the hood. And I say that as someone who's only seen cars on visits to other Earths that have them."

"Thanks for clarifying that," I said.

We all laughed more than the joke deserved. But that's how it goes when you've saved the multiverse together and are about to die.

"So you became part of the Rip?" said Meticulous.

"The part keeping it together," said None of Me. "I was able to nudge it a little here and there for brief periods."

"You sent me to Average's Earth when my portal paper failed," said Meticulous, catching on.

None of Me nodded. "That was about all I could manage. Beyond the note I sent."

"That was a killer ouroboros!" I said.

He chuckled. "I cheated with magic to make that. I couldn't do it myself. That's why I got so excited to find your Stitch, Meticulous."

"You did a brilliant job finishing it," said Meticulous. "But why didn't you launch it?"

"Never finished programming it in time," said None of Me. "The Rip got so bad that I had to pop back up here. I thought I could just lay down a bandage to hold things together and get back to my lab. Instead, I got trapped."

"And that's when you reached out to Mes who could finish the job for you," I said.

None of Me shuddered as if recalling a nightmare. "It wasn't until I saw the Rip from the inside out that I realized how bad the problem was. I knew it was going to take you two working together to really finish the job."

I had a lot more questions, but didn't know where to start. I was too tired to think straight anymore.

"So, you two ready to go?" said None of Me.

"Wait, what?" I said. "I thought we were all stuck here now."

"Which is another way of saying we're about to disappear from existence along with the Rip," said Meticulous.

"You're right," said None of Me. "This place may be fixed, but it's not supposed to exist in the first place. And definitely not now."

"And by my calculations it's about to pop its clogs any second," said Meticulous.

"There's no way out," I said.

None of Me raised a hand, and his palm lit up with green light. "Normally we *would* be stuck here, but the Rip is too busy dying to care about the rules right now."

The air next to each of us folded, and three portals appeared.

I looked through the doorway into Earth Ninety-Nine and saw my room in juvie. Lil Battleship lay asleep on his bed, looking freaked out even in his sleep. I could relate.

If he'd made it back, then Mom, Dad, Twig, and Nash must have made it back too.

Thrilled, I looked over at Meticulous to share the news, but he wasn't in a talking mood. He gazed through his portal into his office, where his version of Dad sat at his desk, weeping as he stared at a holo of Meticulous and Mom in their younger days.

"Well, imagine that," Meticulous muttered to himself. "He does care after all."

"Average, you've been away a night and a day," said None of Me. "Meticulous, you've been away much longer. You two ready to go home?"

"Yes!" we said, jinxing yet again. We looked at each other and laughed.

"I almost forgot!" I told None of Me. "A message from Twig. Your Earth's Twig. She says hey."

The look of hope on None of Me's face was one I promised myself I'd see again the next time I looked in a mirror.

I figured if he could still smile after all he'd been through, then I didn't have anything to frown about.

I wanted to tell him all that and more, but the portals sucked us through before we could so much as say goodbye.

That was okay, though. It might have been a little awkward for all of us anyway.

39

Good Deed for the Day

The very large hands of a very large person shook me awake. "Meade! Meade!"

Lil Battleship?

For just a moment I thought for sure I'd gone back in time to the other morning when I'd sleep-peed on my roomie and he'd needed to save face. Then I saw that Lil Battleship was dressed for breakfast and free of pee. Eardrum and Slime must have already left to go eat.

Lil Battleship thrust out a fist, but it was to bump, not to hit. Then he gave me a quick hug.

"So glad you're okay, bro," he said, slapping me on the back as we pulled apart.

"So where did you end up?" I asked.

Wrong question. His face went tight, and he wouldn't meet my eyes. It was like I'd just asked him about his pet without knowing the pet had died. "You first," he said. "I wanna hear it all."

So I ran him through everything, which actually took less time than I would have imagined. It helped that I'd already practiced telling chunks of the story to my Me friends along the way. Mainly, though, Lil Battleship caught on quickly. He understood my tale better than I would have if I hadn't already lived it myself.

He whistled low when I finished. "Man, and I thought *I* had a crazy trip."

"I'm all ears," I said.

The super-short version was that Lil Battleship, Mom, Dad, Twig, Nash, Caveman, and Barbra the dodo had all wound up on an Earth more or less like our own. The only real differences, in Lil Battleship's mind, were that nobody had thought to invent cheese and they all tended to talk like Yoda. "Not even as a joke!" said Lil Battleship.

He told me how Mom had gotten excited to learn that her old research had been right and there was a multiverse after all. Dad had been thrilled to see that his little Me Co. was a huge Me Corp. there. And Twig got inspired to see her local counterpart writing important stories as the country's leading investigative journalist and documentarian. Nash, meanwhile, freaked out about being so far from home and had a nervous breakdown. Caveman and Barbra wound up babysitting him the whole time.

As for Lil Battleship, his double had died young, but the rest of his family hadn't, and he'd tracked them down. He clicked with all of them, especially his alternate brother, a music producer who uploaded Lil Battleship's music to the internet. His tunes were just getting some serious attention when Lil Battleship got zapped back home. I hadn't realized that fixing the Rip so everything could go back to normal would actually cause my friend harm.

I started to apologize, but Lil Battleship had more news. "So before you woke up, Eardrum and Slime caught me up on what went down here while we were gone."

"By 'caught up' you mean you all had a fight?" I asked.

Lil Battleship smiled for the first time since telling his story. "Nah. We talked, for real. First of all, according to them, you and me are heroes around these parts for our daring escape."

"That's probably the only reason they were nice to you," I said.

"No doubt. But that's just the start. Apparently, the government's launching an investigation into this place. Some *mystery informant* sent over all kinds of online files about the bad stuff they've been up to here."

"Seriously?"

"There'll be a hearing and everything. They're gonna interview us all, so we can dish whatever dirt we like about

O'Fartly and Pooplaski and the rest. They even say our sentences will get reviewed and possibly thrown out on account of all the violations they've already found. Why the weird look? Aren't you happy?"

"Oh, sure. It's just that it seems like a weird coincidence this would happen right after all the weirdness we've been through."

"Yeah, I guess . . . ," he said, trailing off. His mind went elsewhere, probably back to the Earth where he had a lot more going for him than he did here. He'd told me before how he had no idea what he'd do when he got out of juvie, with no family to return to and a bad reputation to live down. That other Earth, though, was a different story.

"So," I said. "You want to go back or what?"

He snapped out of his daze. "What do you mean?"

I felt around for the fizz, which came roaring back. My time in the Rip and a few hours of sleep had fixed whatever damage the origami drive had done to me. Better than fixed—I felt fizzier than ever. I got a vision of the origami key to the Earth where he'd gone, a tube-nosed fruit bat. After folding the shape in my head, I pushed it out just like I'd done before. Lil Battleship's mouth fell open as the portal grew before him.

I didn't know how long this doorway to a different life for my friend would stay open, so we didn't have much time for goodbyes. "Thanks, man," he said, stepping through. "And next time you go sleep-peeing, think of me."

After he left this reality, I noticed the origami octopus

on the shelf next to my bed, just the way Meticulous folded them—decent, but lacking any soul. Well, maybe a little more soul than his earlier attempts.

Inside was a simple note in his writing. Our writing.

You're welcome.

Ours sincerely,
Me

Now I understood. Meticulous had dug up all the dirt on Youth Development while he was sneaking around. He'd even found the time to send all that evidence to the authorities. How had he pulled that off while still hunting down a caveman and a woolly dodo *and* keeping an eye on the Rip?

I had one way of finding out.

The fizz hadn't left me yet, so I focused it on Meticulous. A vision came to me of him standing outside the Me Corp. building. He carried a cardboard box full of origami. At his side in a matching colonial suit, Caveman tried to mimic Meticulous by holding Barbra. The bird was having none of it, squirming and snapping to get free.

Hey, how's it going? I thought at Meticulous.

"Wha?!" said Meticulous, dropping the box.

Caveman hooted in excitement.

"Oh, it's you," said Meticulous. "Nifty trick. When did you develop it?"

Just now.

Meticulous nodded his approval. "Me-to-Me

257

transdimensional communication. Brilliant. Next time, though, maybe you should develop a ringtone so I have the option to pick up or not. Don't get me wrong, I'll probably pick up. Probably."

Fair enough. What's Caveman doing there?

"A cosmic screwup," said Meticulous. "I guess not everything got put back where it came from. We may need to look into that. But in this case, neither Cave nor myself is complaining."

Cave barked in agreement, until Barbra bit his thumb and wouldn't let go no matter how hard he shook. Some pedestrian about to pass them on the sidewalk made a beeline for the other side of the street.

So what's the box for? I asked.

"Oh, I've been kicked out of the building and terminated from my position as CEO."

No way! That sucks!

Caveman and Barbra grunted their agreement.

"Yes, they kicked me out, and Dad too," he said in the same matter-of-fact tone you'd use to recall a walk to the mailbox. "I was away too long, and Dad narked them off by taking a leave of absence to search the world for me. He was right pleased to see me. Rather touching, I don't mind saying."

That's great. You seem pretty chipper about getting fired.

"Oh, it's a relief not to have to run a big corporation anymore," he said. "Don't ever tell her, but some of those things Resist said about big business being rubbish rang true with me. Dad and I are chuffed to start something smaller this time around. Maybe we'll even focus on making things that will help the planet. While turning a handsome profit as well, of course."

Caveman brayed like a mule.

Meticulous grinned. "And you too, Caveman. We're excited about starting over from scratch. And I'm overdue for some family time with Father."

Nice. So what's this about me getting out of juvie? Did you have something to do with that?

"Oh, you know, during some downtime I found certain records that the establishment didn't want found, and I thought the proper channels should see them."

I don't know how to thank you.

"Don't embarrass yourself. Listen, I'd better go. Lots to plan and all that."

Caveman grabbed a few origami from the box and shoved them into his mouth. Barbra snapped her beak at him, demanding her fair share.

Maybe after a little while we can check in again, if you want, I said. *Just so you can make sure I'm staying on the up-and-up, avoiding the life of crime that landed me here in the first place. You can be like my Good Deed Tracker.*

He laughed. "I may be able to clear space in my calendar."

That was as close as we'd ever get to goodbye, but it would do.

I shut off the vision and came back to reality. I felt

drained, but in a good way. As soon as I could, I'd check in on Motor, and Resist, and Hollywood, and every Me I knew, to make sure they'd gotten back all right. I'd try to track down None of Me too. Now that I knew for sure that I could make portals whenever I wanted, maybe I could visit some of them. Maybe we could see about helping Earths, the way Prez wanted.

Maybe I'd even go visit Meticulous.

"This is a good deed," said the MeMinder X.

I called up the menu and deactivated the Good Deed Tracker. Something told me I wouldn't be needing it anymore.

Acknowledgments

Remember those raccoons I mentioned before? The ones who scared me into a state of hyperawareness on my early-morning jog? This time around, I'd like to thank the suburban coyotes who took their place in the predawn wildlife time slot. Just like the raccoons they drove away, these scrappy rabble-rousers helped me dream up some of the ideas in this book, because there's nothing that gets the imagination going quite like stumbling within biting range of a carnivore in the moonlight.

Otherwise, I owe more of my undying gratitude to many other life-forms across the multiverse:

Diane Landolf, who has to be the most patient, understanding, and perceptive editor of at least a hundred Earths, if not all of them

John Rudolph, easily the greatest agent of all the John Rudolphs working as agents across every dimension

Aleksei Bitskoff, an artist so good that I strove to write better in a desperate bid to be worthy of his work

Erin, Wilson, and Oliver, plus the cats, the bearded dragon, and, I guess, the snake too (shudder)

Dani Martineck, Tavia Gilbert, and Dan Zitt at Listening Library, plus all the folks at Penguin Random House Audio

Barbara Bakowski and all the other awesome people at Random House Books for Young Readers

Yoni Brenner and everyone at Lionsgate Films

Matthew, Nicole, Jamey, Kim, Mike, Daphne, Nikki, and Dennis

Mom and Dad, Julie, Debbie, Clay, Skye, Kaley, Ken, Maggie, Willow, Aefe, Steve, Pam, Eric, and Anna

And a special shout-out to my collection of pandemic face masks, which let me walk around in public mumbling plot points to myself out loud without getting the usual looks